find a
PENNY

kennie mae evvie

Paperback ISBN: 979-8-9890589-0-7
eBook ISBN: 979-8-9890589-1-4

Library of Congress Control Number: 2023916737

Published in 2023 by Half Note Publishing.

Printed in the United States of America.

TW: sexual assault and panic attacks. No graphic descriptions.

*To the ones who think they have to fight their own battles.
You are not alone.*

prologue

You never think it could happen to you until it does.

My life was perfect. My parents were happily married. We lived in a nice house. I had a dog and my mom was on the PTA. My sister was popular and beautiful and actually liked hanging out with me. My dad was an engineer and spent the weekends playing soccer with us in the backyard and grilling burgers. I was the winner of the state fair's composition contest my senior year and I had the perfect boyfriend.

Life was perfect.

Then it wasn't.

It's easy to imagine what you would do if everything fell apart. If you lost someone or something. It's easy to come up with these imaginary emergency plans thinking if anything bad ever happens, you're prepared. You're so prepared, in fact, that you know you'll be able to think clearly and make rational decisions when the bad times inevitably strike.

But you're never prepared.

It's amazing how much can change in such a short amount of time. It could be a quick hello or a passing glance. A polite laugh at a terrible joke or a flirty giggle at a corny pick-up line and before you know it your life's turned upside down.

One second, one choice, and everything can change in the blink of an eye.

I'd heard stories about girls like me. I'd watched all the documentaries. I knew it was possible, just not possible for me.

I should've listened to him.

I think about it often - him arguing with me, telling me not to go. Telling me it was a bad idea. Reminding me of all the bad things that happen at parties like that. That's part of the reason I went - to spite him. To prove that I could do things on my own and I wasn't as dependent on him as everyone thought I was. As dependent as I thought I was.

He was the one who found me. I still don't know how he knew where I was. I never called him. I never called anyone. But he knew where to find me. He always knew how to find me.

I never asked how he knew exactly where I was. I never asked him any questions about that night. I didn't want the details. I didn't want to remember any part of it and I certainly didn't want him to remember it.

He took me to the ER, ignoring my constant protesting. I cried and begged him to take me home, but he just lifted me out of the car and carried me inside. I'm glad he did. I was so mad at him for not listening to me and manhandling me into the hospital, but I wasn't thinking clearly. I wasn't rational. My imaginary emergency plans had failed me.

But he didn't.

I finally calmed down enough for the doctor to come in with a police officer to ask me all the questions I'd seen on TV. She asked me so quickly I almost missed it, but she asked again when I didn't respond. She said the words so simply like she was asking me my favorite ice cream flavor. It was the first moment I truly understood what had happened to me. The only time in my life I let myself think about it and remember.

I answered her question after what felt like hours of silence. I said the words I'd never utter again. Words I never thought I'd ever say to begin with. I cried tears I never thought I'd cry.

I cringed from a touch I never thought I'd cringe from.

I saw him out of the corner of my eye, standing against the wall. His leg was bouncing anxiously. He was angry, that much was obvious. I'd never seen him angry. Frustrated? Yes. Impatient? Often. Angry? Never.

Maybe once, sophomore year, when Daniel Lennon said something about me in the locker room after gym. He was livid. It took the entire walk home for me to calm him down. He never did tell me what Daniel said.

But this...this was completely different. His lips were in a tight line, his jaw locked so tight it looked painful. His face was red, and his hands were in tight fists, the knuckles turning white. They had asked him to leave when we first arrived. He'd argued at first, but had eventually obliged. It was only a few seconds later in the stark white room under the florescent lights blurring my vision that I asked if he could come back in.

I just couldn't do it alone.

I probably should've felt humiliated that he was in the room while they examined me, but I wasn't. He made it better.

He made everything better.

It wasn't until I felt his hand on my shoulder that I realized how much everything had changed. His touch was gentle, reassuring. At least it was supposed to be. But as his fingers brushed my shoulder, I flinched before I could even realize what was happening. The look on his face brought more tears to my eyes than I'd cried all night. More than I'd ever cried in my life.

It wasn't him. It wasn't his fault.

But it didn't feel different than what I'd felt just hours before.

Should it have felt different? His touch? Should it have comforted me? I don't know. I've asked myself this question over and over again through the years, wondering if I hadn't recoiled, would we be where we are now. I've spent too many years being angry at myself for not feeling something different when he touched me. I wanted him to comfort me, to hold me, to let me cry into his shirt like I had the Christmas before when my dog died.

I wanted it so bad it hurt.

But everything else hurt worse.

It's easy to look back and see how things could've gone differently. To know how we could've gotten a better reaction or solved a problem quicker. But in the end, if we could go back in time and make all those changes, would we like where it took us? Life is just choice after choice - one small decision after the other until the building of our lives is complete. One small adjustment and the whole building crashes down.

I wonder how I would've handled that one small moment, if I knew what I know now. If I did, would I have listened and stayed home when he asked me to? Would I have made him go to the party with me? Would I have stayed outside or said no when a drink was offered to me? Would I have gone to college, gotten married and lived the dream life we talked about all those years?

Would I have forced him to take me home instead of the hospital? Would I have let him brush my shoulder and hold me through the tears? Would I have stayed after our fight? Would I have told my parents where I was going or called home sooner after I left?

Or, if I could go back and do it all again, would I do any of it differently?

chapter one

then

Charlie Wright was the boy next door.

His family moved in the summer before I started fifth grade. He was going into fifth grade as well. He had curly, dirty blonde hair that couldn't be tamed no matter how much gel his mother used to grease his head. They loosely hung in his eyes, soft curls framing his face. He was beautiful.

I remember when I saw him for the first time.

My mom had met the neighbors while I was at the store with my dad and sister that morning. She'd invited them over for dinner. The doorbell rang at exactly six o'clock. I ran down the stairs and hid at the bottom of the banister to catch a glimpse before they saw me.

I noticed Charlie first.

He was wearing dark wash jeans and a plain blue t-shirt with a baseball hat. There was no logo on the hat, it was just white. Later, I'd learn that he hated logos. Logos on his hats, shirts, shoes. I never really understood why. It was just one of his quirks.

"Penny, come meet the neighbors," my mother motioned to me, and I climbed down the last few steps to stand in front of Charlie. We were the same height, almost exactly.

"This is my daughter, Penny. Penny, this is Charles. He'll be in fifth grade this year, too."

"Hi," I raised my hand in a small waive.

"You can call me Charlie, everyone does," he said with a wide grin, and I couldn't help but smile back.

We had meatloaf that night. I hated meatloaf. There was just something about a loaf of meat that I couldn't get behind. My mom had placed all the kids on the same side of the table. Sandra sat to my right with Charlie's older sister, Kara, next to her. Charlie sat to my left. Halfway through dinner, he caught me sneaking the food off my plate in pieces and feeding it to our dog, Killer.

Sandra had named the dog. She chose the name in hopes of making him seem intimidating, but he was a Pomeranian; nothing about him would ever be intimidating.

I heard a snicker beside me and looked up to see dark grey eyes looking back at me with a smirk on his face. I'd never seen eyes that color before. They almost weren't a color. They looked blue in some lights, green in others.

When it rained, they matched the sky. Maybe that was why I liked the rain so much.

He looked down at the dog then grabbed a green bean off his plate and fed it to him, eyeing the adults at the table making sure he was in the clear.

I liked him instantly. No one else would feed Killer. Mom and Dad said it would make him sick, and Sandra hated the dog. He was supposed to be hers, but he was too messy and loud and would get hair on her jeans as she frequently reminded us. So, he became mine over the years. Mine to feed, to clean, to entertain. We were best buddies. And no one fed Killer but me. Until Charlie.

When dinner was over, my parents suggested we play outside. Sandra and Kara went to the park down the street and were best friends by the time the night was done.

I went straight to the tire swing in the backyard, not checking to see if anyone followed me. My dad had installed the tire swing when I was five. It was a Christmas gift for me and Sandra. We used to take turns spinning each other in circles until we got so dizzy we couldn't walk straight. We'd laugh until our stomachs hurt or until our mom yelled out the window for us to stop before we threw up.

It wasn't big. It was barely big enough for two small people, but Charlie didn't hesitate. He waited just long enough for me to get situated, then climbed in. We sat across from each other; our legs intertwined. It was the closest I'd ever been to a boy.

"What's your dog's name?" he asked as Killer came over and laid on the grass right under our dangling feet.

"Killer."

"That's a dumb name."

"I didn't pick it."

"Good. I don't think I could be friends with you if you did."

"Do you want to be friends with me?"

"I don't know anyone else. Do you want to be friends with me?"

I shrugged. "I don't know anyone else either."

He smiled at that, like he was happy I didn't have any friends. I didn't mind, though. I smiled back.

"Do you take the bus?" he asked as he started to swing us softly from side to side.

I nodded. "The bus stop is on the corner."

"Will you sit with me on the bus?"

I nodded again. "Will you walk with me to the bus stop?"

And so it began.

Our friendship.

Our life.

Our love story.

He knocked on my door bright and early the next morning in a green shirt and the same white hat from the night before. We walked to the bus stop, we sat together on the bus, and my mom had pulled strings that morning to get him in my class.

After that, we were inseparable.

That first school year together was the best school year I'd had at the point in my life. I'd never had friends before. It wasn't as sad as it sounds. I was a quiet kid. I didn't talk much except with my family and even then, I still didn't talk much. Sandra talked enough for everyone.

Sandra and I were only eighteen months apart, so we were at the same elementary school. We would walk to the bus stop together and she would always let me play with her and her friends. I was never alone, but I didn't have any friends of my own.

That first day of school with Charlie by my side was like Christmas morning. I loved introducing him to the teacher and telling everyone he was *my* neighbor, *my* friend. He was mine from the beginning.

Everything with Charlie was new and exciting. He taught me hopscotch and we played on the monkey bars until we had blisters. The second week of school his mom packed him chocolate donuts with his lunch every day that I eagerly accepted when he offered to share. After a couple days I mentioned in passing that powdered donuts were my favorite and the next day he brought powdered donuts to share with me. He only ever had powdered after that.

We spent every day of Christmas break together. We made gingerbread houses, watched reindeer cartoons, and snuck into his backyard on Christmas Eve to see if we could catch Santa Claus on the roof.

I was usually sad to go back to school after holiday breaks, but that year I couldn't have been more excited. The year went by in a blur of powdered donuts, chalked hands, and grass-stained clothes that had our mothers yelling at us as we ran down the hall.

Summer came quickly and by that time our parents had become best friends. They went on double dates on Friday nights, leaving the four kids alone where we would play with the karaoke machine Kara got for Christmas and watch movies our parents wouldn't let us see.

The Wright's invited us to spend the 4th of July together at their lake house that summer at Lake Havasu. They had a house right on the Parker Strip. Their small boat docked right out the back door at their personal dock. It was incredible. It would become a tradition and we'd spend every summer there until our senior year. It was my favorite place to be. There was no school, teachers or schedules.

It was just me and Charlie. Charlie and me. 24/7.

We ate popsicles on the dock and dunked each other under water. We rode our bikes into town to pick-up milk or whatever my mom had forgotten at the store. Sometimes, we would buy ourselves a chocolate bar with the change and share it in the back alley behind the market. We'd tell my mom groceries had gone up in price and snicker as we ran outside to the dock. I think she knew we were buying sweets, but she never said anything.

My parents loved Charlie. I think they were just excited I finally had a friend of my own. Maybe some parents would be concerned about their daughter spending so much time with one boy, but they were happy for me.

Our 6th grade year came and went. We had all the same classes by some miracle, and we ate lunch together. It was as great as the year before if not better. Every day with Charlie was better than the last. It wasn't until the summer before 7th grade that things changed. We got our schedules the last day at the lake and found out we only had one class together. We'd be separated most of the day.

My mom broke the news over dinner, and I'd run outside to the dock in tears. Charlie had come outside shortly after with popsicles. He sat next to me on the dock, our feet hanging over the edge. Our popsicles melted before we could finish, and our hands were sticky, but we didn't care.

"Penny, we'll still eat lunch together every day and walk to the bus stop together."

"It's not the same," I cried, wiping a tear from my cheek.

"It will be exactly the same, I promise."

And he kept that promise. He walked with me to school and sat by me on the bus every day. He still brought me donuts at lunch and would walk with me to the bus stop after school.

7th grade brought more challenges than just a separate classes. Boys and girls were starting to hit puberty and suddenly everyone had crushes. All the girls loved Charlie. They giggled loudly when they walked by him and would ask him to sit with them at lunch, but he always declined. It made me smile every time he told a girl he was sitting with me.

I remember one Friday afternoon a few weeks before Christmas break, we met in the lunchroom, and he frowned. "I don't have any donuts today."

"That's okay."

"No, it's not. I promised you nothing would change, and I forgot the donuts."

It was a promise made weeks ago under duress. I was in tears, he just said what he had to, to make me stop crying. But I realized in that moment, he hadn't broken his promise once. He had sat with me every day and brought me donuts with every lunch.

"Charlie, it's okay. Just bring me twice as many donuts tomorrow."

"I broke a promise, Penny," he looked so dejected, even at thirteen-years-old. He looked like he just confessed to a murder and all he did was forget to bring me cheap powdered donuts his mom probably got at a gas station. It was the first time I saw how much he valued being a man of his word. Charlie said what he meant and meant what he said. His promises were like gold. He never broke a promise and never promised anything he didn't truly believe he could keep.

"You didn't do it on purpose," I smiled and handed him a juice box.

He smiled and we ate our lunch. The next day he brought me twice as many donuts and everything was okay again.

That was the year he started playing saxophone. He joined band and spent most of his time practicing.

"You should learn an instrument too, that way we can be in band together," he suggested one Thursday night in my backyard. He'd just come home from practice and found me sitting in the tire swing, reading a book. I don't even think he'd been home yet. He came straight to me.

"I've never played an instrument before," I said as he climbed into the tire swing next to me.

"I hadn't either, but it's lots of fun. You could play the trumpet or the oboe. The band teacher, Mrs. Jensen, plays the violin. You could try that."

"What if I'm not good at it?" I asked.

"Of course you'll be good at it."

"How do you know?"

He scoffed like the answer was obvious. "Because you're good at everything."

I went the next day to Mrs. Jensen and asked if I could join the band. She asked what instrument I played and I said the first thing that came to my mind. "The violin."

She grabbed a violin from the cupboard and that was that.

I was terrible at first. It was obvious I'd never played before, but Mrs. Jensen hadn't called me out. She simply offered to give me private lessons. We would meet on Tuesdays before school.

"We won't be able to walk to school on Tuesdays anymore," I told Charlie as we climbed onto the bus that day after school.

"Why not?" he asked as we took our seats in the front row.

"Because Mrs. Jensen is going to give me lessons on Tuesday mornings before school."

"So?"

"So, I will have to leave an hour early."

"Okay, but why can't we walk to the bus stop together?" His eyebrows came together in confusion. "There's an early bus on Tuesdays and Thursdays."

"Because I have to leave early. You're not going to wake up an hour early just to walk to the bus stop with me."

"I told you I would walk with you to the bus stop every day and you promised you'd sit with me on the bus," he said simply.

I stared at him in disbelief for a moment before he changed the subject, and we didn't talk about it again. The following Tuesday, he showed up at my door exactly one hour earlier than normal.

"You really woke up early?" I said, opening the door, wide-eyed.

"Of course I did," he smiled.

I think that was when I fell in love with him the first time.

chapter two

now

"Could it be any stuffier in here? And I'm not talking about the temperature." Dannie slides into the chair next to me, her music book dropped lazily on her lap. "These people reek of daddy's money and boring jobs."

She's not wrong, necessarily. Most of these people make more money in a month than I do in a year. That's how you can afford a $120, twelve course meal multiple times a week. Per person.

I started working at *La Mer à Boire* when I moved to the city eight years ago. I didn't have a degree or any experience, I was lucky to even get a job. Most fine-dining restaurants don't really care about your experience as long as you play the right notes, but *La Mer à Boire* is far above 'fine-dining.' I met the owner, Jade Beaufort, randomly at a coffee shop a few days after I'd moved to the city. She'd seen my violin case and asked how long I'd played. Long story short, she asked me to come by her restaurant the next day because her pianist had quit that same morning. It was *le destin,* she'd said. Destiny. Fate.

I didn't believe in fate, but I wasn't going to turn down an opportunity for a job when I was paying for coffee with quarters I'd found in the bottom of my purse. I went the next morning, played a simple Paganini piece on my violin, unaccompanied, and got the job. A few weeks later, Dannie came along to accompany me and we became fast friends. Dannie was boisterous and unapologetic. She said whatever was on her mind, no filter. I was none of those things. Surprisingly, we got along great. We got an apartment together not long after we met.

"If you hate it so much, why do you work here?" I ask.

"Good benefits," she says, rubbing her protruding stomach.

She's five months along and starting to really show. The father's not in the picture, a one night stand she wouldn't be able to pick out of a line up. Her words, not mine.

"They are good benefits, but a lot of places have good benefits."

"Not for musicians," she scoffs.

"Take a break. I'm sure I can do the next set on my own. It's not like anyone is paying attention to us."

La Mer à Boire is an exclusive restaurant. It requires a monthly membership, and that's just to get you through the front door and a drink in your hand. The meals aren't included. We have a few members that come for the bar only, but most dine. Most members are skyscraper executives or doctors. A lot of companies offer membership with employment, it's one of the perks. That's why we have so many people from similar backgrounds.

Dannie and I are the entertainment. It's not as salacious as it sounds, I promise. We're the *musical* entertainment. We usually play four sets a night, starting at 5pm and ending at 11pm. It ruins night life, as Dannie often complains, but I don't mind. I'm not one to go out at night anyway.

"It's the last set of the night, I'm sure Jade won't mind."

"Are you sure? My feet are killing me and I'm so tired."

I nod. "Go home, I'll see you there."

"You're the best," she gives me a smile then bolts out the back door.

"Oh, Penny, there you are," Jade says, coming around the corner. "Where's Dannie?"

"She went home, she's not feeling well. I told her I could finish the last set myself."

"Of course, you can," she gives me a reassuring smile. "But first there is someone who wants to meet you. He keeps going on about the incredible violin player."

"Sure," I say, following her into the dining room.

This isn't unusual. At least once a week someone wants to complement the musicians. It's my least favorite part of the night. I typically offer a grateful smile and a quick thank you after the first complement before they start on the uncomfortable questions – where did you go to school? Who have you studied with? What's your day job? These are expensive people; they expect expensive answers, but I don't have them.

"Here we are," Jade says motioning toward a gentleman in a grey suit at the back table. He's probably in his forties, well built. Definitely a doctor. "Dr. Jones, this is Penny Maine. Penny, Dr. Jones."

"Pleasure to meet you," he says, standing from the table. He holds his hand out for me, and I take it carefully. It's a quick handshake, which I'm grateful for, but I can't help the quick release of air I'm holding when he lets go. Eight years later and I still have a hard time.

It's just a handshake, I remind myself.

"Pleasure is mine," I offer a closed-lip smile.

"I had to find Jade and ask who the beautiful violin player was. I haven't heard such incredible music in years," he smiles in a cocky way, like I should be eternally grateful for the compliment. As if it's worth more coming from him.

"Thank you."

"I used to play trombone in high school, a little in college. I have a colleague who played the trumpet or...I'm not sure, something brass. I'll have to bring him by next time I come in, he'd love it."

"Thank you," I say again, already taking a step back. "I should get back. My set is starting soon."

"Of course, of course! Wouldn't want to keep you."

"It was nice to meet you Dr..." I trail off, like I've forgotten his name. I haven't, but sometimes they need a reality check.

"Jones," he says with a wink.

I give him one last smile before I turn on my heel and back to the stage.

I see Jade say a few more words, then leave the table. Dr. Jones takes his seat and when I catch his eye he winks again. I hate it when men wink. It's arrogant. Most men, I should say. I remember a particular boy who used to wink at me all the time and it never once bothered me.

I place my music book on the stand with a light shake of my head to block the memories and lift the violin to my shoulder. Without Dannie, I can play more fluidly, relaxed. No tempo to follow or harmony. Just me. It's my favorite kind of playing - when I'm not having to answer to anything or anyone. I add ornaments where I normally wouldn't and skip sections I find boring. The composers are probably rolling over in their graves, listening to my changes, but I like them.

By the time the night is up, the dining room is mostly empty, and the busboys are in a hurry to get out the door.

"Hey, did Dannie leave early tonight?" Walker asks, coming out of the kitchen as I place my bow gently in its case.

"Hey, I didn't realize you were still here," I say.

"Yeah, I was trying a new recipe, but..." he glances back at the kitchen wide-eyed, "it didn't really work. Extra clean-up today."

"I'm sure you'll figure it out. Do you need help cleaning?"

"No, it's mostly done. Did Dannie leave early?" He asks again, tossing the towel across his shoulder.

"Yeah, she wasn't feeling well."

Worry coats his features. "Is she okay?"

Walker Reed is part owner of *La Mer à Boire*. He's a long-time friend of Jade's and they opened it together right after he finished culinary school. She was the businesswomen; he was the chef. He is the very definition of tall, dark and handsome. At thirty-seven years old, he stands at about six-feet tall with black hair, combed to perfection and a chiseled jawline that reminds me why all those girls fall to their knees for fictional men.

He's also completely in love with Dannie.

I've tried to tell her, but she refuses to listen. Especially since she found out she was pregnant.

"She's okay, just tired. She'll be back in tomorrow."

I can see the relief in his eyes "Oh, good. Do you want me to walk you home?"

I shake my head. "No, it's okay. I'll be fine."

"You sure?"

"Yeah," I smile softly. "Thanks for the offer, though."

He shoots me a smile before heading back into the kitchen.

I grab my coat, lift my grey turtleneck a little higher on my neck, change flats for a pair of boots and head out the front door. The weather in March is unpredictable in New

York City. Some days you need a sweater and boots, others you could get away with a tank top. It's my least favorite month. I wrap my arms around myself to hold in the warmth and climb down the steps to the subway.

I don't live that far from work. We chose our apartment because it was within walking distance of the restaurant, just a little over a mile. I walk to work with Dannie every day, but depending on the day, I might take the subway. Usually, Walker will join us on our walk home, he lives just a few blocks down from us. But some days, like today, he stays late to work on a new recipe or clean up after one. Dannie would never admit it, but she hates walking alone. I'm sure she took the subway tonight. She's somehow convinced the subway is safer, though I'd strongly disagree. I only take the subway on the days she insists. Otherwise, I'd rather walk.

When I finally make it home, Dannie's door is closed, but I know she's sleeping from the faint snores emanating from her room. I tiptoe to the living room and try to pull out the couch as quietly as possible, wincing when it creaks as I unfold it. She sleeps like the dead, but I still try to be quiet.

After I brush my teeth, wash my face, and climb into bed, I close my eyes and dream of summer nights with sticky popsicle fingers and saxophone players.

chapter three

then

We had most of our classes together in 8th grade and we couldn't have been more thrilled. We sat in the front row for most of them, Charlie's decision, and spent the majority of our time passing notes not-so-subtly. If our history teacher, Mr. Franks, wasn't knocking on one-hundred and senile, we would've been caught and sent to the office. He was our favorite teacher we'd ever had. We got away with a lot because of Mr. Franks.

We joined band again. We had to audition the first week of school and when the sections were posted I'd found my name in the middle of the section. Mrs. Jenson had been the greatest teacher, and I'd come a long way, but I still struggled. I always seemed to be a beat behind. Literally.

"You're just getting better, Penny," Charlie said finding my name on the board.

"I'm in the middle, Charlie," I groaned.

The middle chair was the worst part of the section. No one wanted to be in the middle. The best were in the front, leading the group. The second best were in the back to keep everyone together. Then there were the middle chairs. The ones who needed someone on either side of them to keep them in line. No one wanted to be a middle chair.

"You did great, Penny," he said, taking my hand to lead me toward the bus.

"No, *you* did great. You're the lead saxophonist for the jazz combo."

"Out of two, that's not that impressive," he joked, but I didn't laugh.

"Come on, you're doing amazing! Next year, you'll be first chair, I'm sure of it."

"Easy for you to say. You're good at everything."

"Just because I'm good at the saxophone, doesn't mean you're *not* good at the violin. You've only been playing for a year. You're just going to get better. And you're already the best." I could tell he was exasperated. He hated when I complained about my flaws. He seemed to think I didn't have any.

The school year flew by. It was the busiest year we'd had at the point. We spent most of our spare time practicing our pieces for band. We would play in my backyard, taking turns on the tire swing while the other played. When we were done, we'd eat snacks on the swing and play with Killer until Charlie's mom yelled over the fence that it was time for dinner.

Charlie's family went to visit his grandparents in Ohio for Christmas break. I cried when he told me we wouldn't be together on Christmas. He gave me a tight hug and promised me he would call me every night. He kissed my cheek before he climbed into the backseat of the car. No one had ever done that before. I mean, my mom kissed my cheek sometimes and my dad on my birthdays, but that was it. I stood on my front lawn for minutes after he left, stunned.

He kept his promise. He called me every single night he was gone. I could hear Mrs. Wright in the background almost every night telling him it was time for bed after we'd been on the phone for hours.

When he came home, we were rushed back into band practice. We didn't have much time for anything else. The pieces were hard and eventually we had to practice on our own, realizing we were more of a distraction to each other than help. When the school year came to an end, our concert day approached and I woke up in a frantic pool of nerves. But I quickly relaxed when I went downstairs to find a big blue balloon in my living room that read, "YOU CAN DO IT!"

I didn't have to read the note or see the messy handwriting to know who'd sent it.

I'd wish you good luck, but you don't need it! You're going to do great. – Charlie

I smiled wide and went to the concert with that smile still stuck on my face, nerves forgotten.

That summer my parents went on a cruise for two weeks and sent Sandra and me to the Wright's lake house alone. They were going to meet up with us after their cruise, but it was the first time we'd gone without them. I was a little too excited.

Sandra met a boy that summer and they spent the majority of their time kissing. Charlie and I would gag and complain anytime we came home to find them on the couch.

"One day, you're not going to think it's so gross," Sandra said as she dragged her boyfriend outside. I don't remember his name, but he had a tattoo, long boy-band hair, too many bracelets and was way too old for her. That's probably why he never came to dinner and why she always snuck out after saying she was going to "call it a night" with the fakest yawn. I still don't know how my parents were so clueless. She wasn't subtle.

"Nope. I'm not kissing a girl until I'm in college," Charlie promised.

"Don't make promises you can't keep," I said poking him in the chest.

He snatched my finger and held on tight, wiggling my hand. "I can keep this one."

I rolled my eyes, yanking my finger out of his grasp before running outside toward the water. "Last one in has to do dinner dishes," I yelled behind me.

He beat me, of course, jumping in before I'd even made it to the dock. He was faster than me and I never could take him by surprise. He always knew what I was about to do before I did it. Always one step ahead of me.

When my parents did finally join us at the lake house we already had a routine. Charlie and I spent most nights on the living room floor in piles of pillows and blankets watching movies and eating way too many donuts. At least, I ate way too many donuts. The older Charlie got the less interested he seemed to be in the donuts.

"You've had donuts with lunch every day of your life, Charlie. You don't just stop liking something," I said one summer night as we sat on our pile of pillows watching game shows, licking sticky powder off my fingers.

"Spoiler alert," he said, tossing popcorn in his mouth. "I never liked donuts."

My eyebrows scrunched. "What are you talking about?"

"The first day my mom put those chocolate donuts in my lunchbox was a mistake. They were supposed to go in Kara's lunch."

"Then why has she been putting them in your lunchbox for the last three years?"

He tossed more popcorn in his mouth, his gaze never leaving the TV. "Because you liked them so much. I asked her to put them in my lunch and I switched to powdered when you said they were your favorite."

I sat there, my mouth open, for I don't know how long before he finally turned to look at me. He lifted his finger to my chin to shut my mouth.

"You're welcome," he smirked. And then he winked at me.

It was the first time anyone ever winked at me and I really wanted him to do it again.

Freshman year started strong. Charlie and I had most of our classes together and I did move up one chair in the orchestra which had Charlie shooting me an 'I-told-you-so' look.

High school was a zoo. I felt overwhelmed and confused. Everyone was in a clique, and I didn't fit in anywhere.

"We don't need a clique, we have each other," Charlie said.

It took us a few days of school to figure out the new campus and find a good lunch spot, but eventually we picked a spot in the back of the quad. There was a small table with two chairs under a tree away from most.

"But don't you feel like we should...spread out?" I asked timidly.

"We're not butter," he scoffed.

I just rolled my eyes and ate my lunch.

I didn't spread out much, but Charlie did. He made friends with everyone and even joined the debate team. I still don't know how he found the time for band, debate, spending so much time with me, and still keeping his grades up, but he did it flawlessly.

It wasn't until sophomore year that things started to shift between us. We'd been inseparable that first year of high school. Charlie was growing like a weed, his hair somehow getting curlier every day. He'd passed his awkward years with ease. When he turned fourteen, acne set in, and he started wearing glasses. He hated his glasses. His mom had picked them out and they were frameless, wire-rimmed glasses.

But his awkward phase didn't last long. By his fifteenth birthday in January, his acne had cleared, and by his sixteenth he'd gotten a new pair of black, aluminum rimmed glasses that made his grey eyes pop and accentuated his perfect cheekbones.

He was beautiful.

I was just hitting my awkward phase. I got braces on my fifteen birthday in March and decided to cut bangs on my sixteenth birthday. It was a terrible combination. I had no idea how to do my hair anymore and no color band on my braces seemed to make them disappear.

So, it came as a huge surprise when the week before spring break, a boy in our class asked me to the Spring Fling dance. Andy's family had moved to town right before school started. Being the newest addition to our class, the girls quickly flocked to him. For the longest time he thought Charlie and I were dating.

I remember standing awkwardly in the quad when I told Andy yes. I caught a quick glance over Andy's shoulder to see Charlie far too focused on the mediocre pizza he'd grabbed from the cafeteria.

Andy gave me an awkward one-armed hug that I graciously accepted, my eyes never leaving the back of Charlie's head as he hunched over his lunch.

Charlie was quiet the rest of the day and even quieter on our way home. He usually talked enough for the both of us, which was one of my favorite things about him. There was never a shortage of conversation. I could listen to his voice every minute of every day and never tire of it.

"Are you okay?" I finally asked as we turned onto our street.

He shrugged. Charlie didn't shrug. It was the kind of reaction you got from someone who didn't want to speak their mind or felt uncomfortable. Two things Charlie never felt. I hurried to get in front of him and stopped in my tracks.

"You've been quiet since last period," I asked. "Did something happen?"

"No," he was looking at the ground. Another thing that was out of character. Charlie made eye contact. It bothered me sometimes when we were little, it felt too intimate. But all I wanted in that moment was for him to look at me.

"Why are you so upset?"

"I'm not upset, Penny, let's go."

He took a step around me and started walking faster. I didn't push. I just followed him home, two paces behind. It wasn't until we finally reached our houses, and I was halfway up my porch, that he spoke.

"Penny?"

I turned to find him standing on his own porch.

His eyes caught mine. "Don't go to the dance with Andy."

He didn't wait for a response. He turned quickly, before I could even process what he'd said and went inside. I heard the click of the lock while I still stood on my porch steps, frozen.

I'd never really had crushes on boys. I didn't need to. I always had Charlie. Then, we got to high school and suddenly everyone had a boyfriend or girlfriend. It was normal. People who had known us forever, knew we were just friends, but the new kids assumed we were dating. Like Andy. We never cared enough to correct them, but also, nobody ever actually asked us.

When Andy asked me to the dance, I was shocked. I hadn't ever considered dating and it's like he opened the flood gates and all these ideas started swirling around in my head. Possibilities of holding hands as we walked through the halls and kissing on the front porch as crickets chirped around us.

But none of those fantasies included Andy.

It was Charlie's face I saw in my head when Andy asked me to the dance, and it was rainy grey eyes I saw when I said yes. So, it wasn't hard to climb the three steps to my front door and call Andy to tell him I couldn't go to the dance with him.

In hindsight, it was a pretty terrible thing to do – to call him just hours after I said yes to tell him I was going with someone else. But I didn't care. Honestly, I don't think Andy cared that much. He met some girl at the dance and they dated through graduation.

Charlie never asked me to the dance. Not officially. Some girls might have been annoyed by that, but I liked it. I liked that it was just a given. He didn't have to ask, and I didn't have to say yes. We just...were.

On the way to school the next day I told him I'd called Andy. He nodded once and we didn't talk about it again. Later that same day, during third period, he bought two tickets to the dance.

It was at that dance that we became more than friends. He picked me up and we walked to the gym in our fancy clothes. We danced every dance, I spilled punch on his suit, and he carried my shoes while we walked home. He even walked me to my door, something he'd never done before.

"That was so much fun, Charlie. Thanks for buying tickets," I smiled shyly as we stood on my front porch.

"You look really pretty tonight, Penny," he said. I could feel the heat in my cheeks. He said it so comfortably, like he'd always been calling me pretty.

"Thanks," I whispered, barely able to form words. It was the first time I felt that way about a boy. The first time a boy had told me I was pretty.

The first time I thought a boy might kiss me.

I remember a fleeting thought pass through my mind, wondering if I could even kiss a boy with braces. The thought left my brain the minute he took a tentative step forward and gently placed his hands on my hips. I sucked in a breath and held it. We'd never been this close before. I mean, we'd been close, but not this kind of close.

"Penny," he said carefully, eyes focused on mine. "If I kiss you, will you kiss me back?"

It was so like him to just come out and ask. Straight-forward, honest, bold.

My cheeks grew warm, and I nodded.

He kissed me.

It was a simple kiss. Soft. Chaste.

There was no tongue, our mouths were closed. It was just a light brush of his lips against mine.

And I couldn't have asked for anything better.

He sighed against my mouth, his breath tickling my upper lip and squeezed my hips once before letting go.

"Goodnight, Penny." He grinned as he walked across the yard to his house.

The next night, as we sat on the back porch of his house, I'd remind him of his promise never to kiss a girl all those summers ago and we'd laugh until our lips found each other's, and nothing seemed funny anymore.

chapter four

now

"What were you dreaming about last night?" Dannie asks, stuffing her hands in her coat. It's cold outside, but the pizza place is so small, the three of us wouldn't fit, so we're waiting outside for Walker to pick up our pizza.

It's not uncommon for us to order pizza on our way to the restaurant. We like to get there early and eat some food while Walker starts prepping dinner, before we setup the stage and practice. Sometimes we mix things up and pick-up Chinese, but ever since Dannie got pregnant, it's mostly been different variations of bread and cheese.

"Why?" I ask, confused by her question.

"You were talking in your sleep, very loudly."

"Oh, sorry."

"That's okay, I barely get any sleep these days with this thing kicking me around all night," she pokes at her stomach. "But what was it about?"

I look down at my hands shivering in the cold. "I don't remember."

The lie slips out easily. I remember exactly what I was dreaming about last night. I can still smell the murky lake water and taste the banana popsicles on my tongue and see the white trail behind us from my powdered donuts.

I can still feel his breath on my cheek.

"Really?" she says, pulling me from my thoughts. I look down at my feet to hide my blush. "I always remember my dreams."

"That's because I'm so unforgettable," Walker says coming out of the restaurant with a pizza box and plastic bag.

She scoffs. "If I'm dreaming about you, it's a nightmare I'd sell my upper lip to wake up from."

"Ah, but if you didn't have your upper lip, our dreams together would be far less interesting."

She just rolls her eyes. "What's in the bag?"

"Salad," he says as he leads us across the street to the restaurant.

"Salad? You know you could splurge with us once and just eat the pizza."

"It's not a splurge when you eat it four times a week. Besides, you don't look like this eating pizza, Dannie Lynn," he stands a little straighter and rubs what is likely a six pack under his shirt.

She narrows her eyes. She hates it when he calls her Dannie Lynn. "Right, you look like that from sucking human souls and bottling children's tears. How could I forget?"

He laughs as he unlocks the front door, ushering us inside.

"Have you guys ever said anything nice to each other?" I ask as I take off my jacket and hang it on the hook just inside the kitchen.

"Once, but I'm sure it's happened more in Dannie's dreams," Walker says earning him another eyeroll from Dannie.

"Come on, I'm starving," Dannie groans taking the pizza into the small breakroom just on the other side of the kitchen.

I take my seat across from Dannie as she opens the box and takes a bite of pizza without even bothering with a plate.

"What's your issue with Walker anyway?" I ask as I place a piece gently on a paper plate.

"Nothing, except his insufferable arrogance and pretentious shoes."

"Pretentious shoes?" I ask with an eyebrow raise.

She shrugs, taking another bite of pizza. He does wear a lot of loafers, so I don't argue.

The door from the kitchen bursts open and Jade comes gliding in. "Ladies, it's a beautiful evening and we're completely booked! That's the first night this week we've been booked in advance."

Her smile is soft. Jade would never show too much emotion, but I can tell by the softness in her shoulders and the fact that she hasn't made a comment about Dannie eating like an animal that she's in a good mood.

"That's great," I say with a smile, and I see Dannie mouth "kiss-up" out of the corner of my eye.

I ignore her, my attention still on Jade. "Anyone new or just regulars?"

"A bit of both. Mr. Jorgenson is coming in with his wife and Patti Larsen is bringing her son. He's a doctor of some sort from L.A. He has a podcast or vlog or something, very popular."

She lists off many more names like I'm supposed to know who they are and how influential they are when she suddenly cries, "Oh!"

I jump a little at her exclamation and Dannie shoots a glare her way.

"I almost forgot," Jade continues. "Dr. Jones called this morning and booked two tables for Thursday night. Can you believe it?" She claps her hands together and brings them to her chest. Her eyes practically sparkling. "You must be quite the charmer, Penny."

"That's great, Jade," I say again. Thursdays are our slowest nights, so she has reason to be excited.

"Well, finish up. You need to practice, practice, practice. We must provide the most exquisite environment tonight." She glances at Dannie who has half a piece of pizza in her mouth and her smile fades.

"Really, Dannielle, must you eat like a barbarian?" She scrunches her nose in Dannie's direction before scurrying into the kitchen. Probably to pester Walker about tonight's menu.

Dannie looks at me after the kitchen door swings shut behind her. "If she shoved that stick up her butt just a little bit farther, do you think it would come out her nose?"

I shake my head but can't help laughing.

"Who's Dr. Jones?"

"He was here last night. I don't know if he's been in before, I think he's new. Jade was doing a lot of schmoozing. More so than usual."

She rolls her eyes. "Was he the one she had you meet?"

I nod.

"Was he nice?"

"I guess," I shrug. "He's the same as all the others."

"Pretentious?"

I laugh. "Pretty much."

"I don't know why we have to talk to any of them anyway. We're just the background noise."

"The same reason Walker has to go out so people can compliment the chef. Schmoozing."

"Do you want any more?" She points to the last piece of pizza.

"Nope. All yours."

"Ugh," she groans, grabbing the last piece. "I'm so hungry all the time these days."

"Is that normal?"

"I think so. I read online that your appetite could increase in your second trimester. I hope it's normal. Otherwise, I'm going to balloon into the size of a house."

"You're not going to balloon."

It's comical to think of Dannie ballooning into anything. Even five months pregnant she looks like a model. She's twenty-nine but looks younger. She's tall and lanky with perfect cheekbones, mermaid red hair, and legs for days. I'm pretty sure she's six-feet tall but likes to pretend like she's five-ten. Not sure if she actually cares or just likes to give Walker a hard time when he mentions how compatible they'd be since they're the same height.

"Please," Walker suddenly appears though the kitchen doors, "someone give her something to do. She's trying to change the entire menu!"

He runs around our little table and hides behind Dannie.

"You're thirty-eight years old, Walker," she says, smacking his head. "Stop hiding behind a pregnant woman."

"I'm thirty-seven, thank you," he smirks. "And she won't come near you while you're eating. She'll have nightmares of panda's chomping on baboo."

"Charming." Dannie deadpans.

"Walker, you know how she is," I chime in. "She just wants everything to be perfect."

"And it will be. If we cook what *I* want. I don't know what part of 'Walker is the chef' she doesn't understand."

"Maybe because you're hiding behind a pregnant woman in your own kitchen," Dannie adds.

He flicks her nose and she bats his hand away.

"Technically, we're not in the kitchen. Besides, she – oh crap, she's coming," he bolts again, back into the kitchen.

"Anyway," Dannie turns her attention back to me. "I know you're going to say no, but I'm asking anyway. Kelsey, that girl I was telling you about from my Lamaze class, is having brunch next Saturday at her new house upstate. You should come. There's going to be some single guys there," she waggles her eyebrows at me.

"I have stuff on Saturday."

"Yeah, at one in the afternoon."

I raise my eyebrows.

"You follow a schedule like a freaking clock and we've lived together for almost a decade. Is it so surprising I know you have a weekly appointment at that time? I'm not stalking you."

She throws away the pizza box and turns to me, placing her hands on her hips.

"It's at ten in the morning. You could still be back in time for your appointment."

"I practice in the morning," I offer, though I know it's a weak excuse.

"You can skip it once, Penny. The park will still be there next week."

"I don't know," I try to say, but she's already interrupting me.

"Penny, you can't live the rest of your life in that stuffy apartment. Or worse, this stuffy restaurant with no company but Jade or Walker."

"I like Walker," I point out.

She rolls her eyes. "I'm just saying it will be a simple outing. Some finger sandwiches and mimosas. Just think about it."

She doesn't give me a chance to respond before she heads into the dining room.

I know she's right. I'm not an idiot. I know I shut myself off and I'm anti-social. I know I should put myself out there more, I just don't know how.

My therapist tells me to face my fear by starting small. This would be starting small. It's brunch with Dannie. It shouldn't be a big deal, but everything is a big deal.

When I first left Arizona, I didn't have a plan, I didn't know what I wanted, and I went to the first place I thought of that was as far away as I could go.

I wanted an escape and New York offered me that.

At first the city's population was overwhelming. I hated being touched by anyone and it was rare to go anywhere without bumping into someone. Especially on the subway. It's why I walked everywhere the first few months – fewer opportunities to physically run into someone.

I was so overwhelmed at first that I didn't leave the hotel room I'd rented that first week for three days. Then I met Jade, got an apartment, and things got a little better.

It wasn't until Dannie showed up that I realized how secluded I'd become. I had my routine that I strictly followed because it was comfortable. Because it was reliable. I knew where I was, what I was doing and with who. There were no what-ifs or unknown possibilities. I was in control.

And control was all I wanted.

But at some point, I'd have to let go.

I have to live the life I left Arizona to find.

chapter five

then

Our relationship moved slowly. We still spent the majority of our time together like we always had, but at the end of the night, Charlie would walk me to my door. Whether it be the back door, front door, or my bedroom door, and he'd kiss me goodnight. He'd hold my hand while we walked to school and trace circles on my arm while we ate lunch.

He still brought me donuts every day and practiced with me in my backyard.

We didn't tell anyone. It's not that we intentionally wanted to keep it a secret, but we shifted so seamlessly from friends to more it felt like there wasn't anything to tell.

Sandra was the first to know. It was the beginning of summer before our junior year. We were sitting on the dock, watching fireflies when Charlie leaned down to kiss me.

"I thought you weren't kissing anyone until college," Sandra said from behind us.

She was standing alone, arms crossed, eyebrows raised.

"Mind your own business," I snapped at the same time Charlie joked, "Jealousy's a bad look on you, Sandra."

Sandra just scoffed then left us alone on the dock.

It wasn't until the end of our lake house trip that same year that my parents found out. It's not that they were unobservant, Charlie and I were just subtle. We weren't all over each other. We were the same way we'd always been. He'd kiss me goodbye, always simple, always chaste and hold my hand while we walked to the lake, but otherwise, nothing had changed much. We were also usually alone. My parents trusted me and trusted Charlie. We spent most of our time in the backyard or in our rooms with the doors closed. No one was watching us.

The last day at the lake house, my mom came into my room while I was packing my things.

"Are you and Charlie more than friends?" she asked.

I looked up from my suitcase to find her standing in my doorway, arms on her hips. I don't know what prompted her to ask. Maybe she saw us kiss or holding hands. Maybe she wondered what we were doing behind closed doors all those late nights.

I nodded.

"How long as this been going on?"

"Since the spring fling dance."

"That was five months ago." She didn't yell. She didn't raise her voice, but I could hear the hurt in her tone.

I nodded again.

"Why didn't you tell me?"

I shrugged. "I didn't want to make a big deal out of it."

And that was true. I didn't. After Charlie kissed me for the first time, I was on an emotional high. Floating on cloud nine as they say. But after the excitement wore off, I got nervous. What if we broke up? What if he realized he wanted to date other girls? I was terrified of losing Charlie, he was all I'd ever had. I think that's part of why we moved so slow. I was terrified of running so fast, we wouldn't see the edge of the cliff and fall before we realized what was happening.

"You can tell me anything, Penny," she said gently.

"I know," I smiled.

"So, all the times you've been in your room with the door closed..." she trailed off like she couldn't find the words.

I raised my eyebrows. "What about it?"

"You two are being...careful? Right?"

We stood in silence for a moment before I realized what she was saying.

"Gross, Mom, no! We're not doing...that." I looked anywhere but at her. My cheeks flamed red, and my hands felt clammy.

I hadn't even thought about sex. I was sixteen. I knew of other girls who'd had sex, they talked about it in the locker room after P.E., but I wasn't ready for that. I changed in the bathroom stalls because I didn't want other girls to see me in my underwear. I couldn't imagine getting undressed in front of a boy. Even Charlie.

That was not happening any time soon.

"Oh. Okay. Well, be careful."

"I will, Mom. You don't have to worry about that."

She nodded and turned to leave before stopping in the doorway and turning abruptly to pull me into a hug.

"I'm happy for you, sweetie. That boy adores you."

I hugged her back. "He's the best."

"Good. Because you deserve the best, don't forget that." She hugged me once more then left.

Junior year was my favorite school year we had together. We didn't have as many classes together, but it didn't matter. We spent every minute we could together.

I finally got my braces off right before school started and my bangs had grown out, thank heavens. I'd never forgive Sandra for encouraging me to cut them. My awkward phase was soon behind me and Charlie was getting taller every day. For most of our friendship we'd been the same height, but there were a few years in there I was taller than him. Not anymore. He was a full head taller than me by the start of the school year.

We spent most of our evenings together. We still practiced for band, but most of the time we found it hard to focus on anything but each other. Charlie's hands constantly found me. Whether it was a brush on the cheek or his fingers trailing down my arm, he seemed to always be touching me. My cheeks began to hurt from the constant smiling and my stomach from all the laughter.

He was like a drug. I could never get enough of him.

He still brought me donuts with his lunch. Every once in a while, he wouldn't remember to bring anything. On those days I'd make fun of him for forgetting and then he'd kiss me until I couldn't remember what we were talking about. I think sometimes he "forgot" the donuts on purpose just so he had an excuse to kiss me. Not that he needed an excuse. I would've kissed him for anything at that point.

Our kissing evolved junior year. I don't know exactly what had changed or when, but you couldn't pry our lips apart with a crowbar.

What started as pecks on the cheek or lips became open-mouthed, hands everywhere frenzies. I loved it. I remember the first time his tongue ran across mine, laying in my bed together, I had to push against his chest to catch my breath.

"I'm sorry, Penny," he said, moving away from me, reading everything wrong.

I took his face in my hands and pulled him back on top of me. "No, don't leave. Don't stop. It's just...a lot." I said, lost for words. I didn't know how to describe what I was feeling in that moment. I'd never felt so many emotions at one time. Excitement, joy, lust, anxiety, fear, peace, trust, *hope.*

It was overwhelming.

He laughed once, twisting my hair around his finger. "I know what you mean. Sometimes I can't concentrate because all I can think about is you."

I knew exactly what he meant because in that moment, I couldn't think of anything but him - his lips, his hands, his eyes, his...everything. I remember wishing I could tell him just how much this meant to me, but the words wouldn't come. Instead, I pulled his lips back to mine.

It was the greatest feeling in the world, loving someone that much. I didn't know what it was at the time. I never would've used the word love to describe it at that point. I mean I knew I loved him, but I had always loved Charlie, he was my best friend. I didn't have words for what this was. But it was unabashed, all-consuming love, whether I realized it or not.

Charlie had two solos in band for our Christmas concert and spent more time practicing than ever before. We'd had to graduate from the tire swing since neither of us fit in it anymore. Sometimes we still practiced in my backyard, Killer sitting on our laps. Other times we'd practice in his room because it was almost twice the size of mine.

Sitting on his bed, listening to him play was my favorite pastime. Sometimes he'd grab my violin and ask me to play with him, but I usually refused. Not because I didn't love playing with Charlie, I just liked listening to him more.

"You're making me nervous," he said on a Saturday afternoon, suddenly stopping in the middle of the piece. "Stop watching me."

"I like watching you," I said from my regular spot on his bed.

"Well, it's freaking me out. Read a book or something." He ran an exasperated hand through his unruly hair.

"It sounds really good."

"Not good enough."

Charlie was a perfectionist, to a fault. Everything had to be perfect. Even down to the way his shoes were lined up in his closet. I remember when I first came into his room in fifth grade, I had taken my shoes off and tossed them haphazardly (his description, not mine) by his door. He'd walked around me to line them up neatly without a word. After that, whenever I took off my shoes, I carefully placed them side by side.

He was structured and methodical in ways I'd never seen before. Both of my parents were the fly-by-the-seat-of-your-pants kind of people and Sandra never had plans or a place for anything. He was one of those people that had a routine he strictly followed every single day. He woke up at six every morning and went for a run. He'd take me to Taco Tuesday every week at exactly seven o'clock. He practiced his saxophone every night from seven to eight and he neatly folded his clothes and placed them in his dresser drawer at the end of the day.

I, on the other hand, could not have been more different. I rarely woke up on time, pressing snooze sixteen times. By the time I did roll out of bed, I was rushing to the door after rummaging through the stack of clothes on my closet floor and usually did my makeup on the bus. I couldn't keep track of anything. I lost my house key so often Charlie finally made his own copy.

We only got locked out once, but that was Charlie.

It's why we worked. He directed me when I was lost, and I calmed him when he was frantic.

"Charlie, it *is* perfect. You always play perfect. Why do you think that recruiter called you?"

He looked at me out of the corner of his eye, one eyebrow raised, the telltale sign for 'I don't want to talk about it.'

He'd gotten a call from a Julliard recruit a few weeks into the semester. They saw a video of him playing online and wanted him to come in for an audition. We were all excited. It was flattering to be called, but to be called your junior year? He was practically a prodigy. Something his parents had constantly been reminding him of. He always smiled when they said it, but I could tell it made him uncomfortable and none of it mattered, because even when the recruiter mentioned scholarships, Charlie still declined. When I'd asked him why, he looked at me like it was obvious, and we'd gone on with our ice cream and hadn't talked about it since.

"Charlie, come on, why won't you audition?"

"You sound like my mom," he rolled his eyes, removing his saxophone strap from around his neck and placing the instrument back in its case.

"Well, any time anyone asks, you ignore it or change the subject. Why don't you want to audition?"

He plopped down on the bed next to me and started rubbing his neck.

"There's not enough security in playing. What could I do professionally as a musician? I don't want to teach and if I played for a living, I'd probably have to travel to make enough money and I'd never be home. We'd hardly see each other."

He talked about our future like it was given. It probably was. I rarely questioned whether we would last. I was nervous when we first got together, afraid we wouldn't last, and things would be awkward between us. But it didn't take long for those fears to subside. There would never be anyone for me except Charlie. I think I knew that the moment I laid eyes on him when I was ten – that it would always be us.

"You can do anything you want to do. I just want you to be happy," I said, brushing a wayward curl from his forehead.

"I won't be happy at Julliard."

"Okay."

"Okay?" He raised his eyebrows. "Just like that?"

I nodded and he sighed heavily.

"My mom keeps bugging me, my dad keeps throwing the word Julliard into random conversations...everyone keeps pushing."

"I would never push you into something you don't want, Charlie. If you don't want Julliard, okay."

He kissed the tip of my nose. "Thank you."

"So, what do you want to do then?" I asked, though I already knew the answer.

"I want to go to UCLA."

Charlie had been talking about UCLA since he was kid. Since before I even knew what college was. Both his father and grandfather went there. Also, being the perfectionist and planner he was, he'd been planning college since before he could talk.

Of course, I had no idea what I wanted to do with my life. I thought about ASU, but I'd also thought about a community college while I figured things out. I just knew I wanted to stay in Arizona. I couldn't imagine leaving. I loved Scottsdale, but I also couldn't imagine staying if Charlie left.

"What do you want to study?" I asked.

"I'm not sure yet."

"Well, when you decide let me know."

"You'll be the first to know, Penny."

He kissed my lips quickly before standing up and pulling his saxophone back around his neck. I laid back on the bed, eyes closed, listening.

He never did tell me what he decided. I never brought it up again and by the time we graduated, too much had changed, and our focus had shifted. I always assumed he studied music. He was an incredible musician and he loved it. But I also knew Charlie and he wouldn't do something until he had exhausted every possible outcome and made a list of the benefits and drawbacks from every single option. There were so many things he could do. He was the captain of the debate team, he had straight A's and even tutored some kinds in math. The possibilities were endless for him.

It always bothered me that I never knew what he chose. It was a constant reminder that there was a whole version of him that didn't involve me.

chapter six

now

"Dannie, are you awake?" I knock lightly on her door the next morning. It's already ten in the morning and she's still in bed.

"No," I hear, mumbled from the other side of the door.

"Don't you have a doctor appointment today?"

"Not until eleven-thirty."

"Do you want me to go with you?" I ask as the door swings open, and she stands in front of me with messy hair and no pants. Dannie has no boundaries. She'd walk around naked if I didn't complain.

"You're sweet, too sweet, but no."

I ignore the 'too sweet' comment. "Are you sure? I'm sure it's not fun going alone."

"I'm fine. I'm an independent and capable woman. I can have this baby all by myself," she vows as she walks around me to make the very short walk to the kitchen.

We live in a one-bedroom apartment that we can barely afford. We have a pullout couch that I sleep on, and she got the only room. She offered the room to me when we first moved in, but I politely said no and she didn't push anymore. Honestly, I don't mind. I don't have a lot of stuff and the couch is fairly comfortable.

"I know you are," I say, following her. "Doctors can just be...hard." I swallow pushing the memories aside. "Sometimes it's nice to have someone there with you."

"Doctors don't really freak me out, I'm fine. What about you? What are you doing today?" she asks, grabbing jam out of the fridge for her toast.

"I'll probably go practice at the park."

"Oh right, it's Thursday."

It is Thursday. And every Tuesday, Thursday, and Saturday, I practice in Central Park. It started a few years after I moved here. I went to the park and noticed a few other people playing and it intrigued me. It had to be the most incredible feeling – letting go in a public place with no fear and just playing. It took me a few walks around the park, carrying my violin, before I plucked up the courage to try it. I never was one for performing alone, but once I got my job at the restaurant, I had to learn to like it.

It was far better than I imagined. Playing at the park made performing something I actually enjoyed. I loved it so much it quickly became part of my weekly routine.

The routine Dannie is currently judging me for.

"You could mix it up you know, maybe do something besides practice or read," she licks jam off her finger. "Like brunch next weekend?"

"I like practicing and reading," I argue.

"And that's great, but don't you want some variety?"

"I like my routine," I say, opening a packet of oatmeal.

She eyes the oatmeal - the same oatmeal I eat every morning - with an eyebrow raise. "Anyway, after my appointment I'm meeting some friends for a late lunch if you want to join."

"Thanks, but I'm – "

"Busy," she finishes for me with an eye roll. "If you change your mind, we're meeting at Moynihan at one."

"Thanks, Dannie," I say with a small smile.

"Penny, if you ever want to talk or..." she trails off.

Dannie doesn't know much about my life before we met. I've kept things close. She doesn't understand why I'm so obsessed with my routine and always knowing where I'm going and when. She doesn't understand why I don't like to go to bars on our nights off with her or why I never go out with her friends.

I don't want her to know. I don't want her to judge me or look at me differently. Or worse - feel sorry for me.

I came to New York to get away from that.

I was sick of everyone tiptoeing around, afraid of stepping on shattered glass.

Me being the shattered glass.

"I know," I say with a smile. "Thanks."

She smiles again before heading back to her room. Part of me wishes I could be honest and tell her I can't meet her because I have therapy, but that would open too many doors and raise too many questions that I don't want to answer just yet. That I might never want to answer.

Her door is still closed when I grab my violin and put on a pair of boots before heading out the door. Luckily, I don't live far from Central Park, and I walk most of the time. I'm one of the few that walk without earbuds. I like the sounds of the city and the people, but mostly I like being able to hear my surroundings.

My phone rings in my pocket and I see my sister's name before I answer. "Hey, Sandra."

"Hey! How are you today?"

She's asked me this exact same question every time I talk to her. Not 'how are you', 'how are you *today*'. It's like she thinks one day I'm going to wake up and suddenly feel different. Or be different.

"Good. You?"

"Good. I was hoping I'd catch you. Figured you were on your way to the park."

I ignore the mocking voice of Dannie in my head noting that even my sister, who lives on the opposite side of the country, knows my routine.

"What's going on?"

"What do you mean 'what's going on'? It's your birthday. I call you every year."

"Yeah, I was hoping maybe you'd forget this year," I mumble as I cross the street into the park.

"Still hate your birthday then, huh?"

"I don't hate it. I just don't know what I'm celebrating."

"Life."

What life? I want to ask, but I don't.

"Happy birthday, Penny."

I groan.

"Come on. Say thank you. Smile. You're twenty-seven, this is the most exciting time of your life!"

"Thank you," I say reluctantly.

"Have you heard from mom or dad?"

"Dad texted me this morning, like he usually does. I haven't heard from mom."

"Well, it's still early, she's probably not awake yet."

"Yeah, I'm sure she'll call."

She's silent for a long time and I'm pretty sure I can hear the sound of her tapping her nails on the table. A clear sign she's nervous.

"Was there something else?" I ask.

"I have news," she says quickly, her breath slightly ragged.

"Is everything okay, Sandra?"

"Yeah, everything is fine."

"Then why are you freaking out? What's the news?"

"Okay. I'm just going to say it." She takes a deep breath. "I'm getting married."

This might not sound like a big deal to most, but considering I didn't even know she was dating anyone, it's a bit of a shock. I stop dead in my tracks on the sidewalk, my mouth hanging open.

"To who? When?"

"His name is Lucas. We're getting married in June."

"Wow. Congratulations," I finally manage, forcing a smile on my face in hopes she'll hear it as I start walking toward the park again. "I'm so happy for you."

"Really?" She sounds slightly less tense, but not completely relaxed.

"Why wouldn't I be happy for you?"

"I don't know, we don't talk much, and I never really told you I was seeing anyone seriously," - more like she never told me she was seeing anyone, period - "and I just...I'm really excited, Penny, and I hope you'll come. To the wedding, I mean."

"Of course, I'll come. I wouldn't miss your wedding day, Sandra."

"Well, we're getting married in Arizona. Scottsdale to be exact."

And there it is.

"Oh."

"Yeah," she sighs, and I can hear the understanding in her voice, almost feel it through the phone. It's one of the reasons I avoid calling home so often – I'm sick of hearing the pity everyone still carries around on my behalf. Sandra is better than my parents. My mom always has this whine in her tone like I'm a lost puppy she has to find a home for. My dad mainly communicates via text, because I don't think he knows what to say to me.

Sandra is the one I can still count on. The one who has never been afraid to push me with tough love. But occasionally, that tone comes out and I'm that sad, lost, eighteen-year-old girl again.

"I know it's a lot to ask, but I wouldn't ask unless it was really important."

"I know," I say. "Why Scottsdale?"

"Lucas is from here, too."

"Really? Did you know him from school?"

"Yeah, he was one grade above me. We ran into each other at a conference in L.A. and hit it off. Once we realized we'd gone to school together things moved pretty quick."

"I'm so happy for you."

"Thanks. So, will you come?"

I want to say yes. I want to be able to go to my sister's wedding and worry about nothing but making sure her makeup doesn't smear and hold her dress while she uses the bathroom. But life isn't that simple.

"Can I think about it?" I close my eyes tightly, not wanting to hurt her feelings. It's something I started doing after I graduated. If I closed my eyes tightly enough, I would disappear. No one could see me. I knew it wasn't true, but it's how my brain coped. After a while, it just became a habit anytime I felt uncomfortable.

I can hear her sigh in disappointment. "Of course."

"Thanks. Look, I gotta go, I just got to the park."

"Yeah, no worries, I'll talk to you later. Happy birthday, Penny." She hangs up before I can respond and my quiet 'thanks' hangs in the air.

I look at my phone until the screen goes black.

Scottsdale. I haven't been back since I graduated. I left three months after graduation and never looked back. I hadn't even told my parents I was leaving. I left in the middle of the night with my violin and a backpack. There was too much baggage and history in Scottsdale that I just couldn't face, good and bad.

I find my usual spot in the park, the far west side near an Elm tree, and grab my violin. I play a few notes before it hits me. It's been a few months since I had a panic attack. Honestly, I thought they were gone. It'd been almost a year. The last one had been in the bathroom of a bakery in Brooklyn when I saw a penny on the floor.

I can usually guide myself out of them. I don't know if it's because they're not that bad or because I've grown accustomed to them. Maybe both.

At some point I'm aware of a lady asking me if I'm okay and I'm able to nod my head and mumble an, "I'm fine." I don't know how long it takes, but eventually my vision clears, my breathing normalizes, and I'm on my knees leaning against the tree. I'm sure I look completely insane, but it wouldn't be the first time someone thought I was odd.

I gather my violin and bow back in the case, the moment ruined. I'll need the extra time to get myself together before my therapy appointment anyway.

I walk quickly, this time with my earbuds turned loud enough to drown out my thoughts.

But the memories always find their way in.

chapter seven

then

I was having a panic attack. At least, I thought that's what it was. I'd never had one before. My chest felt tight, my breathing ragged, and my legs were going to give out on me any second. I stood on the side of the stage just inside the curtains behind a giant Christmas tree where I couldn't be seen but could still see the crowd. The brass section was taking their leave and I had a few seconds before I had to take my place in the front, but there was no way my feet were going to carry me all the way across the stage to stand front and center before the crowd of hundreds. It was a miracle I hadn't fallen over yet.

"You're going to do great, Penny."

Charlie's hand squeezed mine and I gripped his fingers tighter than necessary. He was wearing a bright red sweater with a reindeer coming out of it. It was Mrs. Jenson's idea to wear ugly Christmas sweaters for our concert. She thought it would "mix things up." I thought it looked like Santa's elves had thrown up on the stage. But I had to admit, even in a hideous red sweater, Charlie was still the most beautiful thing I'd ever seen.

"Don't break my hand," he laughed. "I still have to play my second solo."

"Sorry," I said, pulling my hand from his abruptly.

"You're going to do fine. Take a deep breath."

Charlie had already played his first solo and it had been flawless, of course. He'd bowed and smiled then rushed backstage to check on me. His second solo was the last piece of the night, after the strings. The first few pieces had been a jazz combo, which was where Charlie's solo came in. After that, the brass quintet played a couple pieces and then the strings were to come out for a few numbers before the entire band gathered to play the last song of the night.

Jenna Lance was supposed to play the solo for the first string piece, but she was currently puking her guts out with food poisoning.

"I didn't prepare for this," I mumbled, wiping sweat from my forehead.

Mrs. Jensen had come to me a few weeks ago after class and asked me if I would learn the solo "just in case." I didn't think anything of it. Everyone had an understudy of sorts. Brandi Lyle learned Charlie's solo in case something happened and he couldn't play.

But nothing ever happened. Every year two people were assigned the same solo, but the backups never played. There had never been a need.

Until Jenna Lance decided to eat fifteen-day old chicken she'd found in her college boyfriend's fridge. Now I was about to pass out, staring at the giant crowd waiting for me to make a complete fool of myself because of some rancid bird.

Life could be so cruel.

"Penny, you've practiced this song for weeks. I've heard you play and it's beautiful." He kissed my cheek. "You're beautiful."

I gave him a side-eye glare, before glancing down at my own ugly sweater that had a cow dressed in an ugly Christmas sweater on it. It was a sweater within a sweater, Charlie had joked when he found it at the thrift store.

He laughed. "Okay, cow sweater aside, you're beautiful."

He moved behind me and started rubbing my arms. "It's okay to be nervous."

"I've never done a solo before."

"I know."

"What if I forget?"

"You won't forget."

"But what if I do?"

"Then you mess up. Everyone messes up. It doesn't mean you aren't good." He kissed the top of my head.

I turned around to look him in the eye. To say thank you or kiss him I hadn't decided when I suddenly heard Mrs. Jensen's voice over the loudspeaker.

"Ladies and gentlemen, thank you again for coming out tonight. The students have been working very hard, as you heard during the first – "

I didn't hear anything else she said, my stomach had jumped right out of my body and onto the floor. I was going to pass out. At least Charlie was here to catch me.

"If I pass out, catch the violin first. I could never tell my parents they have to pay for a new one because I couldn't keep my wits about me enough to actually play it," I joked, but it fell flat.

He chuckled. "Noted."

"I can't do this, Charlie," I said, shaking my head aggressively.

"Penny, look at me."

I did as he asked and met his charcoal eyes.

"I love you."

His voice didn't waiver.

His eyes never left mine.

He said it like he'd said it a million times before.

I stood there, mouth agape, unable to move. I was faintly aware of students rushing past me to take the stage. A blurry sea of violins, cellos and violas. Mrs. Jensen must've introduced us.

Charlie just smiled a devious smile like he knew exactly how he'd affected me. He turned me gently and gave me a tiny shove toward the stage where I walked carefully, completely unaware of the crowd staring at me.

Mrs. Jenson looked to me for confirmation that I was ready to play. I'm sure I looked like a dear in the headlights, but I nodded my head once and suddenly the music started. I listened carefully for my queue and when the time came, I started playing.

And I played perfectly.

All at once I forgot what I'd been stressed about, I couldn't remember that feeling of my stomach falling or the fear of passing out. All I could think about were those three little words and that perfect smile.

It hit me halfway through the song why he'd said it when he did. He knew I needed a distraction. He knew I needed to think about nothing but playing.

And with his words sitting front and center in my head, it worked. It was like I was playing in my backyard with just Charlie while he played fetch with Killer. As if we were in his room, just the two of us, playing piece after piece, laughing, and eating stale donuts.

There was no one else in the room except us.

It was the first time I realized how much I loved playing. How much I loved losing myself in a piece of music, forgetting about everything and everyone except the notes on the page and the feeling it gave me. It was the first time I thought I could do this forever.

When the song came to an end, I nodded my head in a gracious bow as the crowd clapped and cheered, before taking my seat with the rest of the strings to play through the remaining set list.

Once we finished and were ready for the final number, I watched as Charlie sauntered onto the stage with the rest of the band, his eyes never leaving mine until he took his place in the front with the rest of the soloists and all I could see was the back of his head.

That final number seemed to last forever. All I could think about was Charlie.

I watched him more than I watched my sheet music. I don't even know what notes I played. Thank heavens I wasn't the only violinist.

When it finally came to an end and we all found our way to the band room to put away our instruments, my eyes searched the room frantically before I caught sight of Charlie talking to one of the tuba players in the back. I moved quickly, practically running, shoving through anyone who got in my way. I ran into his arms before he realized I was coming. He tumbled over, flat on his back laughing as I landed on top of him.

"I love you, Charlie," I said, lifting my head to look at him.

His hands moved up and down my sides as he smiled.

"I love you more," and he kissed me right there on the floor of our band room with everyone cheering and laughing.

We had a big dinner after the concert. Mrs. Wright made fried chicken and my mom made apple pie. We gathered in the Wrights dining room, our parents making us play our solos again for the family.

We played charades and the Wright's won, as they usually did. We ate crunchy apple pie while my mom apologized profusely, not realizing she was supposed to cook the apples before she put them in the pie.

Later in the night our parents gathered in the dining room to reminisce about their own high school days, Mr. Wright telling stories of when he played trombone in band. I leaned over to rest my chin on Charlie's shoulder.

"Come outside with me," I whispered.

He took my hand with a smile and pulled me outside.

"Thank you for today," I started as we walked down his porch steps, hand in hand. "I never would have made it through that performance otherwise."

He kissed my cheek. "Anytime."

"You did mean it, right?" I asked as I opened the side gate to my backyard.

He tugged my hand to make me face him.

"Of course, I meant it."

"You didn't just say it to get me out of my head?"

"No." His finger lifted my chin to meet his eyes. "I mean, I hadn't really planned on saying it right then. I kind of blurted it knowing it would get you out of your head."

He laughed once before taking my face in both of his hands, his face suddenly serious. "But I still meant it, just the same."

I lifted up on my tiptoes to brush my lips against his.

"I love you, Charlie."

His smile widened, bigger than I'd ever seen. "I like the sound of that."

I giggled as I pulled him into my backyard where we took turns on the tire swing, kissing, laughing, and kissing some more. By the time we finally went inside my house, the moon high in the sky, our families had gone to their respective houses and my parents were already in bed. We tiptoed up the stairs to my room being careful not to wake anyone. We didn't brush our teeth, we didn't change our clothes. We kicked our shoes off, climbed into my small, twin sized mattress and fell asleep.

I woke up the next morning to the feel of Charlie's lips on my neck and the whisper of a promise.

"I'll love you forever, Penny."

The summer before our senior year were some of the happiest days of my life. My family spent the entire break at the lake house just like we had every year before but this time it was different. Our parents had set more ground rules now that Charlie and I were officially dating. At least, now that they knew we were dating. No more late-night walks at the lake, we both had curfews. No more hanging out in our bedrooms with the doors closed.

So many rules.

Sometimes we would remind them we were almost eighteen and were practically adults, but one "humph" from his mother and a glare from mine had us nodding our heads and agreeing to their terms.

Until they went to bed.

Charlie would sneak into my room after everyone was asleep and he'd hold me while I slept. I'd wake up to his lips on my cheek, my neck, my hand, my back, before he'd sneak out before anyone woke up.

He never asked me for more than sleep and I was grateful. I loved Charlie, more than anything, but I wasn't ready for that step.

On July 4th, we piled blankets in the back of the beat-up grey truck his grandpa had given him for his sixteenth birthday and headed into town to get provisions. Charlie drove with one hand on the wheel and the other tracing circles on my bare thigh. I was dressed for the holiday in a red, white, and blue sundress that had a halter top and stopped mid-thigh. It wasn't my favorite dress, but by the look on Charlie's face when he saw me in it, it was definitely his.

"We're running late, so we have to be fast," he said as he parked the car outside the market.

"I already know what I want."

"Let me guess, powdered donuts," he grabbed my hand as we met in front of his truck.

"Don't judge the donut. Especially when you're probably going to get something annoyingly healthy like walnuts or a protein bar," I rolled my eyes.

"Do you want me to maintain these abs," he joked, rubbing his stomach that definitely *didn't* have a six pack. I laughed as he opened the front door but came to a stop when something shiny caught my attention on the floor.

"Look, a lucky penny!" I said as I bent to pick it up off the dirty gas station floor. "For you." I held it out to him, but he shook his head.

"I can afford snacks, thank you," he scoffed.

"It's a lucky penny."

"What does that mean?"

"What?" I practically shouted. "You don't know what lucky pennies are?"

His eyebrows came together. "Should I?"

I rolled my eyes even more aggressively and began to recite. "Find a penny, pick it up, all day long you'll have good luck."

He looked at me like I'd lost my mind.

"So, it's a lucky penny." I held it out to him again. "For you."

"No thanks."

"But I want you to have it."

"I don't need it," he shook his head.

"Why not?"

"I already found my lucky Penny." He shot me a cocky smile, then grabbed my penniless hand and pulled me toward the donuts.

I smiled the whole drive to the lake and curled my body around his during the firework show. I think it was the happiest I'd ever been. I'd never felt so loved, treasured, adored. When the firework show was over, I reached up and pulled his face to mine. We kissed more that night than ever before and a part of me never wanted to stop. But after what felt like hours, he pulled away.

"Please," I practically begged, tightening my grip on his hair.

"You're making this really hard, Penny," he groaned as his hold tughtened on my hips. "I'm trying to be a gentleman."

"I don't want you to be a gentleman." I tried to pull him back to me, but he wouldn't budge.

"I'm not making love to you for the first time in the bed of my truck in the middle of the woods."

"But you will?" I whispered. "Someday?"

He reached up to brush my bottom lip with his thumb and nodded. "I promise."

His promises were like the warmest blanket on the coldest night, and I wrapped it around myself. "Don't make promises you can't keep," I joked.

He laughed. "This is one promise I can guarantee I won't break."

"I want you to be my first," I said quietly.

"I will be."

"You promise?"

His eyes were shining in the moonlight, looking almost silver as they stared into mine. "I promise."

And we kissed some more until the smoke from the fireworks was gone and the only sounds besides our ragged breaths were the crickets at the lake.

chapter eight

now

"Where is your brain tonight?" Dannie asks me as we walk through the dining room for our fifteen-minute break Thursday night.

"What?" I ask.

"You seem really distracted tonight. More than usual at least."

We find our chairs in the break room, and she pours herself a cup of tea.

"I guess I just have a lot on my mind."

That's the understatement of the century. Therapy was useless. I was frustrated and exhausted and barely said a word. Dr. Grand was as patient with me as ever, but days like today make it hard to find use in my ongoing therapy appointments.

"Well, get it back in here. You were playing so fast I could hardly keep up."

"Sorry," I start, but Jade interrupts us.

"Penny!" She waves her hands dramatically like I can't see her only six feet away from me. "Dr. Jones is back tonight and is hoping to speak with you."

"Tell him to find a new toy, this one's taken," Dannie says and Jade glares.

"One of these days Dannielle, that mouth is going to get you into trouble."

"It already has," she scoffs with a glance down to her stomach.

Jade opens her mouth to retort, but I cut them off. "Let's not keep Dr. Jones waiting."

Jade finally nods and I follow her into the dining room. Honestly, I don't know why Dannie still works here. She hates it, Jade hates her and I spend most of our breaks keeping them away from each other. I'm almost positive the only reason she's still here is because of a particular chef she insists she can't stand.

"Aw, there she is. The shining star!" I hear Dr. Jones before I see him.

"It's lovely to see you again," I smile as we approach the table. He's seated at a larger table than last time, but only two other men sit with him. I give them a smile and notice the empty table settings are messy and the chairs pushed out, so he must have brought a full table of guests.

"I brought some colleagues tonight. I told them how lovely your music was, and they insisted on joining me."

"That's very kind of you. Thank you."

"I was going to introduce you to one of our newest members," he starts, glancing around the room, "but he's running a little late." He gives me another smile and motions to the seat next to his. "Please, sit with us. I'll get you a drink."

I shake my head. "Oh no, I couldn't. I'm supposed to be back on stage in just a few minutes.

"Oh, Penny," Jade chimes in. "I'm sure you could go on a little late."

I raise my eyebrows. Jade would lose her mind if I ever went on late. I swear she counts the seconds and if I'm off by just one, she's already yelling into the kitchen asking where I am.

"We had them bring us a round earlier, there seems to be a few left." He takes a full glass from the table and holding it out to me.

"No, thank you," I say with a light shake of my head, maintaining my polite smile.

"Oh, I insist. I'm sure Jade wouldn't mind." He winks and the knot in my stomach tightens. It's obvious he's buzzed. Maybe not drunk, but one more drink and he very well could be. Walker has pushed Jade for a drink limit, but she refuses.

I don't drink alcohol and I don't take drinks from strangers. Especially from drunk strangers. It's one of the main reasons I don't go out with Dannie. Bar hopping isn't that much fun without a drink in your hand.

"You're very kind, but I can't. I don't drink."

He laughs like I'm making a joke. His words slightly slurred when he says, "Everyone drinks." He shoves the drink closer to my face.

I can smell the alcohol and my eyes start to go blurry. "I'm sorry, Dr. Jones, but I just don't..." I fumble over a chair as I try to turn my attention elsewhere.

"Come now, it's just one drink – "

"She said no, Walt."

Time stops.

My lungs stop.

My heart stops.

Everything stops.

"Charles, finally!" Dr. Jones eyes the man behind me. "This is the violin player I was telling you about."

My feet won't move, and I can't seem to get my lungs to cooperate. The panic attack is bubbling under the surface, and it takes all my concentration to keep it at bay.

"Penny." He breathes my name more than says it. I've only heard him speak so softly once before and I can't handle those memories right now.

I close my eyes tightly and think back to all the things I learned in therapy over the years. I take deep breaths and count.

In...two...three...four, hold.

Out...

"Penny, are you alright?" I hear Jade say beside me. I nod softly and open my eyes. Everyone at the table is looking at me like I've lost my mind.

Maybe I have.

"Excuse me," I mumble and turn on my heel toward the kitchen without looking at him, but I can feel his eyes on my back as I practically run out of the dining room.

I'll feel better once I get outside. The dining room isn't small, but I feel confined. Trapped.

"Penny, you're late, Jade is going to freak – what's wrong?" Dannie says as I bump into her on my way through the kitchen doors. I see Walker in my peripheral vision, saying something with a worried look in his eyes, but I can't hear him.

I do hear another voice behind me saying my name and the pounding of footsteps following me into the cool night air, but I ignore it and rush through the back doors.

Once I'm outside I take a few deep breaths until I feel like I'm in control again. But then I hear the door open, and I know it's him. He doesn't say anything, he doesn't close the distance, but I know it's him. I'd know him anywhere.

Don't be a coward, Penny.

I take one more deep breath and then another. Then one more before I finally force myself to face him.

It's like an arrow to the heart.

He looks exactly the same.

He looks completely different.

His blonde hair is cut shorter than I've ever seen, you wouldn't notice the curls unless you knew to look for them. It's darker too, not nearly as blonde as it was when he was a kid. His glasses are larger than he had as a teenager, but the rims are smaller. He has a faint beard, which shocks me the most. He was always clean shaven as a teenager. His facial hair came in earlier than anyone else in our grade, but he always shaved.

He's wearing a pair of navy dress pants with a cream button down and the sleeves are rolled to his elbows. I can't help but notice he's wearing the tie I got him for our senior prom. I bought it to match my prom dress. It's lavender. I know it's the one I got him because I can see the small etching on the bottom.

Our initials.

For some reason this brings me back to reality and I manage to speak.

"Why?" It's the only word I can get out. I have so many questions.

Why are you in New York? Why are you in this ridiculously expensive restaurant? Why did Dr. Jones call you his colleague? Why did you follow me outside? Why are you wearing that tie?

He doesn't answer, he just looks at me with a mix of shock and wonder in his gaze. His eyes rake over me slowly and I can almost feel his stare burning my skin. I suddenly feel somewhat embarrassed that I don't look better. My chocolate brown hair is in a low, slick bun and I'm wearing all black. Black sweater, black jeans, black flats. It's my standard work attire. I'm not supposed to draw attention to myself. I'm supposed to be the background noise, not the show. Not that my casual attire is much different. My style never quite evolved. It's usually jeans and a t-shirt, maybe a sweater when it's cold outside.

"Penny," he says when his eyes find mine again. He seems to be at a loss for words as well. All he's said is my name since he saw me, and I hate the way it makes me feel.

Sad, lonely, beautiful, hurt, angry, joyful.

My mixed emotions are wreaking havoc on my brain function and all I can do is stare back.

Neither of us speaks for what feels like hours before I finally manage, "Why are you in New York?"

"I work here."

"Where?"

"Walt Jones office."

"You're a doctor?"

"Psychologist," he clarifies.

"You're a therapist?" My eyebrows come together, and he smiles slightly at my disbelief. He never talked about being a therapist. It's never something I would've pictured him doing. Charlie liked to work with his hands, he liked moving. I can't picture him sitting in a chair in some stuffy office with tissues on every surface asking people about their feelings.

He only nods. "How long have you worked here?"

There is a moment of hesitation before I answer. "Eight years."

I can see the questions in his eyes and the answer I just gave him – where I've been all these years.

"Do you like it?"

I only nod.

I've pictured what this meeting would look like. I wondered what would happen if I ever ran into him somehow, though the odds were against it. I never imagined he'd move to New York. I figured I'd have to go back home, I never thought he'd leave Arizona. He always planned on going back after school. Once of the reasons I left was because I knew he never would.

I clear my throat uncomfortably. "I should get back inside. I'm late for my last set."

"Oh. Of course."

I don't move and neither does he. He's still standing in front of the door to the kitchen. I don't know how he even got back here. Walker or Dannie must've seen him go through the kitchen and should've kicked him out.

He seems to understand my hesitation and takes a step to the side, allowing me access to the door. I take a few tentative steps and stop when he reaches out and holds the door open for me. He's so close, I can smell his cologne. It's different than what he wore in high school, and it catches me off guard. I look up to see his eyes already on mine.

Rainy skies.

I allow myself a few more moments before I turn my attention back to the task at hand and walk through the kitchen acutely aware of him trailing behind me.

He left.

There is a part of me that's disappointed. I thought he would be the last to leave once the night was done, waiting to catch me when I left. High school Charlie would've given anything to see me again. I guess I'm not the only one who's changed.

The dining room is empty. Dannie and Walker left, but not before asking me if I was okay after I played terribly during our last set. I couldn't focus on the music when my gaze kept passing by the head of short curls standing out in the crowd like a sore thumb. I brushed off their worries and they walked out the door together.

I wasn't ready to go home and face reality, so I told them I wanted to stay and practice. It's not unusual for me to do that. I sometimes stay late to practice in the room. It's good to practice with the same acoustics I play in every night. If I'm being honest with myself, I've been hanging around to see if Charlie was just in the bathroom or waiting in the back.

He wasn't.

I'm just putting my violin in its case when my phone rings. I take a deep breath and mentally prepare myself before answering.

"Hi Mom,"

"Happy birthday sweetie!" she practically sings.

"It's one in the morning, it's not my birthday anymore."

"It only ten here, so it's still your birthday!"

"Thanks, Mom."

"Have you had a good day?"

"Yeah, it's been...a day." That's an understatement.

"Have you heard from Sandra?"

"Yeah," I say as I throw my flats into my backpack and slip into my boots. "She told me about Lucas."

"Oh, honey, I'm so glad. Are you coming to the wedding?" I can hear the hopefulness in her voice.

"Um, I, uh...I told her I had to think about it."

"Oh." Her excitement immediately deflates, and I feel terrible. I don't want to hurt my family. I just don't know how not to.

I close my eyes tightly. "I want to be at her wedding Mom, it's just..."

"I know, sweetie. She understands," she says it in a comforting way, like I'm still that same broken piece of glass she's trying not to step on.

Kathy Maine has always been overly understanding. My mother was the kind of mom who patted our backs and told us it was okay to cry. She held our hands when we were scared and told us it was okay to walk away when we were afraid or uncomfortable. My dad often said she coddled us. Dale Maine was the toughest guy you'd ever meet. He was the one that didn't hold the back of the bike but let me fall off over and over until I got it right. He was the one that told me when life throws punches, you throw punches right back.

Sandra got my dad's personality. She's strong and sure of herself in ways I'll never be. "A force to be reckoned with," my mom always said. I had more of my mom in me. The patient, quiet one, but even my mom has a powerful streak I didn't inherit.

I shut off all the lights and head out the front door, checking it's locked behind me.

"So did you do anything fun for your birthday?" she asks as I turn around to find an all-too-familiar gaze staring at me from the curb just outside the entrance.

He stayed.

I think my heart actually skips a beat.

"Penny? Are you there?"

"Yeah,...uh, I gotta go," I say.

He stands and takes a few steps closer, while still keeping his distance. His hair is messier than before, the curls a bit more prominent. It looks like he's run his hands through it a few times since I saw him earlier.

"Is everything okay?"

"Yeah, its...fine. I'll call you later."

His eyes haven't left mine since I came outside.

"Okay, well, happy birthday, sweetie."

"Thanks," I say, before hanging up.

"Hi," he says.

"Hi."

He takes a tentative step forward. "I didn't mean to interrupt your call."

"That's okay. It was just my mom."

"You still keep in touch?" he asks. He seems confused, but there is a small smile on his lips like the news makes him happy.

Of course, he knows. He was there when I left. I'm sure he knows exactly how long it took for me to finally call home after I left.

"A little."

"Good. That's really good."

We stand in silence for a moment, both unsure what to do next.

"You played beautifully tonight."

"Thanks," I say quietly.

He opens his mouth to speak and then closes it. He stares down at me for a solid sixty seconds before he finally decides to speak.

"Look, if you don't want to see me, I completely understand. If you tell me you never want to see me again, I'll walk away." He takes a small step forward. "But I can't leave tonight without asking if I can see you again." He says it so simply. So straight-forward and direct. So...Charlie.

I didn't realize how much I missed it.

"So, can I see you again?"

I might regret it, who knows, but my heart speaks before my brain does.

I nod.

He sighs with relief. "Can I take you home?"

My whole-body tenses and he takes notice immediately.

"Unless you'd rather I not know where you live," he says, instantly understanding, which makes me even more tense. How is it that after all this time he can still read me so easily?

It's not that I don't want him to see where I live, but...I haven't brought a man to my apartment before and who's to say I will see him again after tonight? If I bring him home with me and we never see each other again, I'll never be able to be home without seeing him on that darn porch every time I walk through my front door.

"Do you want my phone number?" I ask and he takes his phone out before I even finish.

"I still have your old one."

He holds his phone out to me and I'm careful to take it without my fingers brushing his. I can tell he notices the awkward grip, but he doesn't say anything.

"I changed my number after..." I trail off and he nods.

"I know."

I search my name in his phone and find it's still under *My Lucky Penny.* He never changed it. I look up to catch his eye and he offers a small smile. If I didn't know any better, I'd think it was a shy smile. But Charlie isn't shy. At least my Charlie wasn't shy.

But this isn't my Charlie. He's not my anything anymore.

I change the phone number and hand it back to him. I'm grateful when he's just as careful not to graze my fingers before tucking it back into his jacket pocket.

"It was really good to see you, Penny." His smile is wide, excited. Hopeful.

"You, too."

"So, when I call you, will you answer?" he asks as he takes a few steps backward, a teasing gleam in his eye.

My retort comes back without effort, like the last eight years haven't happened and we're still making jokes on the tire swing. "Only if you type the number in right."

His smile widens into a full grin, and I find myself offering the smallest hint of a smile back.

"I'll call you tomorrow."

I shouldn't ask. He owes me absolutely nothing, but I can't help myself. "Promise?"

He smile falters for just a fraction of a second and he stops moving. "I promise."

He stuffs his hands into the pockets of his pants, and I turn the opposite direction toward my apartment.

"Penny?"

I turn back to see he hasn't moved. "Yeah?"

"Happy birthday." He turns away then, leaving me frozen on the street.

chapter nine
then

I was never a fan of birthdays, until I met Charlie. I was shy and awkward. I hated the way everyone sat around you and watched you open presents and how you'd have to sit there with a smile while everyone sang to you. It was completely unbearable. My parents realized on my fifth birthday that the normal celebrations weren't for me and they stopped forcing parties on me. My mother was devastated. After that, we just ordered pizza and played board games. It was my favorite way to spend my birthday.

Then Charlie happened.

The first birthday we spent together was my eleventh birthday. My mom let me invite him over for pizza and games with the family. I didn't think he'd bring me anything, but he did. He got me a Walkman.

"I found it at a thrift store with my mom," he said. He had also bought me a CD of the New York Philharmonic with it, and we sat side by side on my tire swing, listening.

For my twelfth birthday we went miniature golfing and Charlie bought me a neon green golf club with all the money he'd saved raking leaves that fall. That was the year my parents bought me my own violin. Once I opened it, Charlie asked me to play something. I was nervous and shy, but I played the song we'd been working on in band for the family after we ate our pizza.

Charlie's family was out of town for a family reunion for my thirteenth birthday and he was sick for my fourteenth.

Two days before I turned fourteen, Charlie left school early with a terrible headache. I didn't see him for three days.

"I'm sorry I'm missing your birthday," he said over the phone. I'd never heard him sound so weak before. I didn't like it. Charlie was the strongest person I knew, even at fourteen.

"That's okay, we can celebrate next week when you're better."

"But next week isn't your birthday."

"Well, you can't come over."

"I know, but we can still celebrate."

"What do you mean?" I asked, eyebrows together.

"Un-scrunch your eyebrows and go look on your porch."

"My eyebrows are not scrunched," I lied as they scrunched further.

He laughed a little then coughed as I made my way down the stairs to the front porch where a small brown box with a poorly tied red bow was waiting with my name on it.

"Charlie, what did you do?" I said, my tone laced with excitement as I grabbed the box and put it on the kitchen counter.

I opened the brown box to find homemade chocolate chip cookies that were slightly burnt, and a movie I'd never seen before. It looked like an action movie.

"You said you'd never watched an action movie before. If you put it in your DVD player and we hit play at the same time, we can watch it together," he said.

I wasn't a big fan of movies, the only ones I watched were sappy romances that usually had Charlie gagging, but Charlie loved movies and I loved that he wanted to share this with me. I smiled so big as I grabbed the cookies and movie and bolted to the living room.

Once I had the DVD ready and the remote in hand, we counted to three.

"One, two, three." We hit play at the same time and sat on the phone while we watched the whole movie together.

I don't remember what movie we watched or how the cookies tasted, but I remember Charlie's voice on the other end of the phone. It was my favorite birthday.

Until I turned eighteen.

Charlie had something big planned for my eighteenth birthday but told me it was a surprise and to stop asking questions anytime I tried digging for details. By that time, we'd been officially dating for almost two years, and he'd been dropping hints for weeks that he had something special planned.

He picked me up at exactly seven o'clock and kissed me quickly on the cheek before leading me to the car.

"Where are we going?" I asked as I climbed into the passenger seat.

"It's a surprise," he said with a wicked smile that had me blushing.

We drove for a while, never getting on the highway. It was getting darker, and I had no idea where we were. I wasn't the greatest at directions. I later learned he drove around in circles for fifteen minutes so I would get confused and wouldn't know where we were going.

"I don't like surprises," I said as we climbed out of his truck in a dark parking lot and his hands went around my eyes.

"You'll like this one." I could hear the smile in his voice as he led me who knows where.

"Will I?" I grabbed onto his wrists, but he wouldn't budge. There was a time in our childhood where I was stronger than him, or at least as strong as he was. But as we grew and he slowly became a man, the dynamics shifted. I found myself enjoying the fact that he could literally hold something over my five-foot-seven head and I couldn't reach it. Or how he'd hide something behind his back and I couldn't get his arms to move. He was just over six-feet tall. He was strong and confident.

"Maybe." He smiled against my cheek.

I laughed. "I wanted a quiet night in."

"Well, I didn't." He nudged me slightly to the right and I cried out when I stubbed my toe on something hard.

"Sorry!" he said, sending me in another direction.

"Are we at the park?"

"Stop asking questions, you'll see in a minute."

"It's my birthday, shouldn't I get to decide what we do?"

"You did decide what we're doing."

I wasn't sure what he meant by that, so I shut my mouth and let him guide me. It was a perfect night. March in Arizona was beautiful. I loved that my birthday was in March. It made it easy to be outside. Sandra's birthday was in the middle of August which kind of limited what we could do to celebrate.

Charlie guided me forward a few more steps before he suddenly stopped, and I was pulled back into his body.

"Are you ready?" he whispered in my ear sending a shiver down my spine.

I nodded quickly and he kissed my neck softly before lowering his hands to my waist.

It took my eyes a minute to adjust to the dark. We were outside, that much was obvious from the smell of ducks and muddy water that I caught a whiff of the second we got out of the car. It took me a minute, though, before I realized exactly where we were. It was one of our favorite places. Most of our dates were spent walking hand in hand down the canal or eating packed dinners near the fountain.

Soleri Bridge.

"What are we doing here?" I asked, my voice high with excitement.

"I couldn't really afford to take you to Paris, so this will have to do," he said, and he nudged me forward until we were in the middle of the bridge and a small flock of ducks swam below us. He reached into his pocket and took out a lock and key. He held it out to me, and I could see our initials etched onto the front.

"I know you'd dreamed of *Pont des Arts*, but you'll have to use your imagination."

I suddenly remembered a night just a few weeks before. We had watched some sappy movie where they went to Paris and put a lock on the bridge. Charlie had never heard of that before.

"What's the point?" he'd asked.

"The point is, it's romantic. You write your names on a lock, hook it to the bridge and throw the key in the river. It's a sign of everlasting love."

He hadn't responded with words; he'd just kissed me.

My eyes shot to his as we stood on the bridge. He smiled wide as he took the lock and hooked it to the steel cable.

"The cable will have to do since the bridge is made of concrete," he said as he clicked it. "And for all I know, this is totally illegal, so we'll have to be fast."

I laughed and he handed me the key once the lock was secured on the cable.

"Happy birthday, Penny," he said, wiping a tear from my cheek. I hadn't even realized I'd been crying.

"Charlie..." I started, words escaping me.

"I love you, Penny." His forehead fell to mine. "So much."

We'd said I love you before. More times than I could count. But something about the two of us on the bridge with the key in my hand was different.

"I love you, Charlie."

He took my face in his hands and gently pressed his lips to mine. He moved slowly, carefully, until I wrapped my hand around the back of his neck, gripping his hair and he moved his hands to my waist, holding tightly. His lips pried mine apart and I melted in the taste of him.

He pulled away suddenly.

"You have to throw the key in the water." His lips were puffy and his hair messy from my hands, but he was the most beautiful thing I'd ever seen when he smiled at me like that.

I held the key tightly for a moment before I turned toward the water and tossed it as far as I could.

Charlie moved behind me, wrapping his arms around my waist and resting his chin on my shoulder.

"I love you, Penny June Maine," he whispered against my neck. "More than anything."

It was an overwhelming feeling – loving someone that much. Especially at eighteen. Sometimes I didn't even understand how to manage my feelings for him. I was young and naïve and dazed half the time.

But standing on that bridge, his lips against my neck, and our bodies pressed together, I knew nothing could ever break us apart.

chapter ten

now

"What happened to you tonight?" Dannie asks as I close the front door behind me.

"Nothing," I say as I kick off my shoes and place them neatly by the front door. "Why are you still up? You should be sleeping."

"I'm fine. I had to stay up to hear about this so called 'nothing'." She shifts herself onto her knees on the couch. "You bolted through the kitchen like a bat out of hell. You looked like you were going to pass out. And then some random guy, who looked like a freaking Greek god by the way, comes running behind you, calling your name."

"You know, when a stranger goes running through the dining room and into the kitchen, you should probably call security."

"Not relevant. Who was the blonde god?"

"He was..." My friend? Ex-boyfriend? What is he? My mind and heart are still reeling from the entire day, I'm not sure I could form a coherent sentence if I tried.

"He's not the one who..." she trails off, eyes wide.

"Who what?" I ask, not sure what she means.

"Who...assaulted you." She's looking me dead in the eye asking me this very personal question, but I can see a slight hesitation in her expression. It's very Dannie to just come out and ask the uncomfortable or inappropriate questions no one else would ever think to ask. I don't know if I'm surprised that she figured it out or not. We've lived together for a long time.

"How did you know?" I ask quietly, after minutes of silence.

She lets out a relieved sigh. "I just started putting things together. You never talk about the past, you don't like any movies or TV shows about romance, you don't like when men touch you, you're weird about drinking and parties." She shrugs one shoulder. "It all just started adding up."

"Oh," is all I say as I fall onto the opposite side of the couch.

"So, was it him?"

"No!" I shake my head aggressively. "He was...uh...he helped me a lot. After."

"Oh. How long as it been since you've seen him?"

"I haven't seen him since I left."

"Is that why you moved to New York? I've always wondered," she asks, resting her arm on the back of the couch, twisting to face me.

I nod. "I just needed to...get away."

"Did he come to the restaurant to see you?"

"I don't think so. He works with Dr. Jones, the guy Jade introduced me to the other night. He brought some of his colleagues to see me play. He was late, though, he showed up right before the last set. I don't think he knew I was the one Dr. Jones was talking about."

"So, now what?"

"I don't know," I sigh, resting my head on the back of the couch. I have absolutely no idea what comes next. I never planned for this. "I honestly never thought I'd see him again."

I left knowing I was leaving everything and everyone for good. I'd accepted that and moved forward the best I could.

And I'd almost forgotten about my sisters' phone call this morning. I throw my hands over my face with a groan and close my eyes tightly.

"What?" Dannie asks.

"My sister called this morning," I say, turning my head to face her. "She's getting married."

"Is that a bad thing? I mean, obviously marriage is," she waives her hand dismissively. "Just your sister in particular."

"No. I'm happy for her, really, it's just...she's getting married in Scottsdale. Our hometown."

"You haven't been back since..."

"No. I haven't."

Her eyes widen. "Well. You've had a pretty big day."

I laugh humorlessly. "You could say that again."

"What about this guy? Are you going to see him again?"

I sigh, twisting my hair around my finger. "I gave him my phone number.

"Do you think he'll call?"

"I know he will," I say confidently. "He promised."

I hate plastic chairs. Who thought it was smart to use a few pieces of measly plastic to hold up an entire 150-pound body?

My normal support group is much bigger than the one I'm currently sitting in, but I decided to go to the Friday morning meeting needing a little extra support after the last two days I've had. There are a few familiar faces, but most are strangers.

"What about you, Penny? Anything you want to share with the group?" Benson asks from his seat at the top of the circle.

I clear my throat. "I've had a couple panic attacks the last week. It's been a while since I had one. I thought they were getting better."

The groups were formed by my therapist, Dr. Grand. He organized the group with a friend of his who teaches at Columbia University. Psychology students with the university usually lead the groups. They alternate, depending on their school schedules. Today is Benson, which is one of the reasons I decided to come. He's my favorite leader.

"Do you want to tell us what happened?" Benson asks.

I shake my head.

"You don't have to share anything you don't want to," he assures me.

"I guess I just thought I was getting better," I say quietly.

"A panic attack doesn't mean you're not getting better. It could be a permanent side effect of your trauma."

"You know," Lisa pipes in beside me. "I used to have panic attacks all the time. Almost every day. It's not so bad anymore. I still have them sometimes, but maybe three or four times a year instead of a week."

"You still have panic attacks?" I ask, surprised. Lisa was attacked almost twenty years ago.

She nods. "I think it's like Benson said, it's just a permanent side effect. Though, it's a lot better now."

"How did it get better?" I ask.

Lisa is in her forties. She is one of the regulars in my Saturday group. I was surprised to see her here today but also relieved to see a familiar face. She was abused by her father growing up and then attacked when she went to college.

She thinks for a moment before she speaks. "I used to think about it all the time. It was on this constant loop in my head. I couldn't work for a while because thinking about it made me physically sick. It wasn't until my little brother moved back to the city that things got better. He was the only man who made me feel safe.

"I got a full-time job and would call him whenever I started feeling sick. He would talk me out of it. He didn't even talk about anything important. Sometimes he would tell me about something funny that happened at work or what projects he was working on. He just wanted to get my mind off of it. It worked."

"Why do you think that is, Lisa?" Benson asks.

"Because I couldn't do it alone. No matter how hard I tried, I couldn't get out of my own head. I needed someone to literally pull me out. He did that for me," she smiles. "I mean, that's why we're all here, isn't it? Because we need help."

She looks at me then, like she knows I'm the one that needs to hear it most.

"It's okay to ask for help. Sometimes that's the only thing that will make anything better."

I offer a smile in return, but I don't say anything. How do I tell her the only people I could ask for help are the same people I can't burden with my problems?

chapter eleven
then

"Charlie, it's fine, I promise. Nothing is going to fall out, let's go," I said for the tenth time. He'd spent the last twenty minutes double checking everything was in the back of his truck, and he wasn't missing anything.

"I just want to make sure this weekend is perfect," he said, and I could tell he was running through the checklist in his brain.

"Charlie, it's two nights, we have more than enough," I said, motioning to the truck bed that was practically overflowing.

He gave me a side eye glare then sighed. "I'm sorry, I just want everything to be perfect," he said, wrapping his arms around my waist.

"Everything will be perfect." I lifted my arms around his neck and kissed his jaw.

After many hours of convincing, our parents had finally agreed to let us go up to the lake house alone. It was late April and we were only a few weeks away from graduation. Charlie had officially received his acceptance letter from UCLA. We weren't surprised, we all knew he was brilliant; his GPA was above a 4.0. I still don't understand how that was even possible, but what did I know? My GPA was barely 3.0. It was the most exciting thing that had happened to us and we wanted to celebrate at the lake house. Just the two of us.

His parents were the hardest to convince, surprisingly. My parents trusted Charlie with their life and apparently with mine.

"This is the first weekend just the two of us, I want it to be – "

"Perfect, I know," I cut him off. "If you say that word one more time, I'm going without you. Everything's going to be great, but we need to leave now before our parents change their minds." I darted out of his arms, and he laughed as I climbed into the truck.

"Hurry up, we still have to pick up road trip snacks," I said, clicking my seatbelt into place.

"I already did." He pulled a grocery bag from the back seat.

"Powdered donuts?" I asked as I snatched the bag from his hands.

"Of course."

"What else is in here?" I started rummaging through the bag with excitement. He'd brought me lemonade and him an energy drink and, "A protein bar? Really, Charlie? You're supposed to eat junk food on road trips."

"I think you eat enough junk food for the both of us." He wasn't wrong. I loved crappy foods.

"What's this?" I asked, making a face as I pulled out a jar of trail mix.

"You can un-scrunch," he laughed, taping my forehead once with his finger. "There's no raisins in it. It's just peanuts, cashews, and chocolate candies."

He spun the wheel with one hand as he pulled out of the driveway. I took a moment to appreciate his forearm before I responded.

"Where did you find it? I'm always looking for trail mix without raisins and it doesn't exist!" I opened the jar and shoved a handful into my mouth in the most ungraceful way I possibly could.

"It came with raisins," he said, pulling onto the highway.

"What do you mean?" I mumbled with a mouth full of food.

"I picked them out."

"What?"

"I picked out the raisins," he said simply, eyes still on the road. "Don't worry I washed my hands first."

"I'm not worried about your germs, Charlie, this is a thirty-six-ounce jar," I stared at him in disbelief.

"I know," he said, turning on his blinker and checking his blind spot.

"Why did you pick all the raisin's out?"

He looked at me like the answer was obvious. "Because you don't like them."

It was that day that I knew I would be with Charlie for the rest of my life. Because I didn't think there was any other boy in the world who would pick out the raisins.

We pulled up to the lake house far later than planned. Charlie blamed me for requiring too many bathroom breaks. But we eventually made it a little after midnight. He parked his truck in the driveway and climbed out quickly to meet me on my side.

He grabbed my hand to help me out of the truck, practically yanking me from my seat. I looked into his eyes to make a snarky remark about him being in such a hurry, but his gaze was heated, desperate and focused only on my mouth. I licked my lips, my heartrate climbing. His eyes shot to mine quickly then once more to my lips before he pulled me up the porch steps. He fumbled over the lock on the front door for minutes, hours, *days.*

When we finally heard the click of the lock, he sucked in a sharp breath, and he pulled me in after him. His lips crushed mine before the door was even closed.

I reacted instantly, throwing my hands into his hair, his tightening on my waist as he pushed me back into the door. He was aggressive in a way he never had been before. He held me up against the door with his whole body, there wasn't a single part of me he wasn't touching.

His lips moved to my jaw, my neck, my shoulder and up again.

"We're alone," he whispered, his voice raspy.

I laughed breathlessly. "We've been alone before."

He lifted his head to meet my eyes. "Not like this."

He was right. He snuck into my room all the time at night, but my parents or Sandra were always just down the hall. We were truly alone here. We had the entire lake house to ourselves for two whole days.

I still couldn't believe our parents let us do this. I mean, we were technically adults, but we were still in high school, and they were still our parents.

"So, what do you want to do?" I asked as his lips moved down my throat again.

He chuckled. "This," he said and I felt his tongue graze my collarbone. I gasped softly; my hands so tight in his hair I'm surprised I didn't pull any out.

His lips found mine again and he gripped my waist tighter, turning us around and moving me back toward the hall. He must've lost patience with how slow I moved because his hands slid down to my thighs and he lifted me effortlessly, my legs wrapping around his waist.

He walked us down the hall and up the stairs, eventually dropping me on his bed and I pulled him down on top of me.

He moved his hands to either side of my head, holding himself up to look me in the eye.

"I didn't plan on this," he said softly, his entire demeanor changing in an instant. An expression crossed his face so quickly I almost missed it. I could've easily mistaken it for fear, but Charlie wasn't afraid of anything. Especially not me.

"What?" I asked.

"I don't want you to think I just brought you here to have my way with you."

I laughed. "By all means, have your way."

He grinned. "Oh, I plan to, but we don't have to rush anything."

"What are we rushing? We've been together since we were, like, ten," I laughed.

He lowered himself down to his elbows. His finger started tracing circles on my temple, his gaze on my lips and his voice soft when he said, "I just want to make sure you're ready."

My fingertips grazed his cheek. "I wouldn't be here if I wasn't, Charlie."

"I love you," he whispered, dropping his forehead to mine. "I need you, Penny."

He finally let me bring his lips back to mine. He moved slowly, all desperation gone. His lips moved languidly with mine and his hands were soft as they reached down to pull my legs around his waist. We kissed for what felt like an eternity, taking our time with each other before I felt him sigh against my mouth and pull away with a flushed face and messy hair.

"I should get everything out of the car," he said breathlessly.

"The car?" I mumbled, dazed from his kisses.

He didn't say anything, he just kissed my cheek softly before untangling himself from my arms and legs. He disappeared out the door before I could even figure out what had just happened. I lay on the bed, alone and confused, for a few minutes before he came back with my bag. He offered me a small smile before he went back downstairs, not saying a word.

I wasn't sure what to make of what was going on. Part of me wanted to go downstairs and demand to know why he told me he needed me then left me five minutes later. But I wasn't sure I wanted to know the answer.

I made my way to the bathroom instead where he'd already put my toiletry bag on the counter. I brushed my teeth, washed my face, and changed into my pajamas. A very purposefully bought matching set of silk shorts and tank top.

It was supposed to be sexy. Because I was supposed to have a weekend *alone* with my boyfriend. Charlie may not have planned on anything happening, but I definitely had. Sandra snuck a box of condoms in my suitcase after I told her my plan. I figured Charlie was on the same page as me.

Apparently not.

I shut off the bathroom light and went into his bedroom to find it still empty. It was late and I was exhausted from driving all night. I switched off the bedroom light as well, not sure when or if he was going to join me and climbed under the covers with a frustrated sigh. It was just a few moments later that I felt the bed jostle and he climbed in behind me, wrapping his arms around my middle and pulling me flush against him.

He must've gotten ready for bed downstairs because his breath was minty fresh, he was wearing basketball shorts and he wasn't wearing a shirt.

His breath swept down my neck. "I love you, Penny."

He started the same circles on my temple again, and I fell asleep to the sound of his breathing.

The weekend was wonderful. We swam in the lake and rode our bikes into town like we used to when we were kids. He bought banana flavored popsicles at the market for us to eat on the dock and he held me the next two nights as we slept. Only slept.

It wouldn't be until later that I'd appreciate him stopping us that night. I wasn't ready and he knew it, even when I didn't. I loved Charlie, but if we'd had sex that night, I'm not sure I'd have been okay with it in the morning. I was young, desperately in love and I knew nothing about real life. I wasn't ready for the consequences of that choice, good or bad.

And he was right, what was there to rush? We had our whole lives ahead of us.

chapter twelve

Thirty minutes. That's how much sleep I got last night.

After the late night at the restaurant Thursday and the support group yesterday, my mind's been racing nonstop, memories coming and going. Also, Dannie snores. I'm staring at the clock when it changes to 7am and I hear Dannie's alarm go off. She must have an appointment. She never wakes up this early.

"Morning," she grumbles as she shuffles out of her room and into the bathroom, closing the door behind her before I can respond.

I've been laying on my back, staring at the ceiling for hours. It's probably not normal how long I can go without moving. I force myself to sit up and my muscles ache from all the tension I've been carrying since I left work.

I'll call you tomorrow.

Promise?

I promise.

I've replayed the conversation in my head a million times. Of course, he'll call. He would never break a promise. But this is eighteen-year-old Charlie I'm thinking of. He's not that person anymore. Just like I'm not.

My phone lights up with a message and Sandra's name lights up the screen.

Her wedding.

In Scottdale.

I throw my body back on the mattress and pull the pillow over my face with a groan.

Sandra and I were always close. We never argued much, she always shared her toys with me. She'd let me tag along with her and her friends when we were little, always afraid I would feel left out. I think she was a little sad when the Wrights moved in. Her and I had always been two peas in a pod and then Charlie came into my life, Kara into hers and we had new best friends.

Of course, we were still close. We'd talk late at night and share all the gossip we heard at school. She'd call me often after she graduated high school and moved to California to tell me all about college and what I had to look forward to.

This should be an easy decision. For most people it probably is. You go to your sister's wedding, you drink too much champagne, you catch the bouquet, and you hug her before she heads off into marital bliss.

Unfortunately, I'm not most people.

I open my phone to read her message.

Sandra: I'll understand if you can't make it.

I know it's supposed to help me or make me feel better, but it just makes it that much harder. She shouldn't have to be the one making all the sacrifices. And Sandra isn't one to coddle me. If she's telling me she'll understand, it's because she's genuinely concerned about me.

"You look like crap," Dannie says, plopping down on the pullout next to me.

"Gee, thanks," I mumble and sit up.

"Did you sleep at all last night?"

"A little. Why are you awake so early?" I ask.

"I have an appointment at nine to meet with a potential nanny," she says with a yawn. "What's on your schedule for the day."

"I'm not sure," I say, and she gasps. "What?"

"I'm sorry, did Penny Maine just say she doesn't have a *plan?*" Her hand goes to her chest, her eyes wide with shock.

I wasn't always such a planner. That didn't happen until after graduation and I moved to New York. It happened subconsciously. It wasn't until I started going to therapy that I realized it was a coping mechanism. Constantly wanting to know where I was going to be when and with who. I like to think that I've gotten less rigid over the years, but Dannie would strongly disagree.

Dannie is the most spontaneous person I know. I don't think she's ever planned anything a day in her life. She often reminds me life is better when it's a surprise.

I hate surprises.

I roll my eyes at her as I nudge her off the bed. She climbs out carefully, her protruding belly getting more difficult to work around with every passing day.

"I have a lot on my mind," I say, pushing the bed back into the couch.

"You have had a pretty crazy couple days," she agrees. "Do you know what you're going to do?"

"Not at all," I say, fluffing the pillows on the couch.

"Well, if you need a plus one, I'd be happy to go the wedding with you. Or if you'd rather sit here and eat your feelings, I'm down for that too."

I can't help but smile. She may be frantic and a teeny bit crazy, but she's the best friend I've had in years. "Thanks Dannie, but it's in June. You'll probably be in labor."

"Labor? Am I pregnant?" she says looking down at her belly. "I forgot," she mumbles, and I laugh.

"I'm going to shower, good luck," she blows a kiss in my direction before closing the bathroom door behind her. I finish folding my blankets and stacking them next to the couch before I make myself oatmeal. I'm just rinsing out the bowl in the sink when my phone rings. It's not loud. My ringtone is always on the lowest setting, but the adrenaline that's been pumping through my veins all night jumps into high gear. I drop the bowl in the sink with a loud thud and ignore the soap bubbles as I practically run to the phone.

Unknown caller

That doesn't mean it's him, I tell myself. Anyone could be calling me. Maybe they're calling to tell me my car warranty has expired.

I take a deep breath and hit accept.

"Hello?"

I hear a sigh of relief before he says, "Penny?"

"Hi," I say, quietly.

"You answered." It's not a question. More just a statement of surprise.

"My phone rang."

He laughs. "I hope it's not too early."

"Not at all. I'm an early riser."

"Really?" There is genuine surprise coating his tone.

It takes me a minute to realize why he would be surprised. I never woke up early when I was a teenager. At least, I didn't get out of bed early. I wasn't usually one to sleep super late, but a few weeks after he started spending the night with me, I woke up to him sneaking out of my bedroom. He was trying to be quiet so he wouldn't wake me. I remember after he'd tied his shoes and grabbed his phone, he'd leaned down to kiss my forehead and whispered, "I love you." Even when he thought I was asleep, he still said he loved me and kissed me before he left me. After that, I never wanted him to know I was awake before him, afraid that I would miss his lips on my forehead. He must've always thought I just liked to sleep in.

"Anyway," he says after a moment of silence. "Do you have plans today?"

"Um, tonight. I work Saturday nights."

"What about this morning?"

I shake my head, even though he can't see me. "No."

"Will you get breakfast with me?"

I could say no. I could say no, never talk to him again, and go on with my life.

But when have I ever been able to say no to him?

"That sounds nice."

I hear a sigh, like he was holding his breath. "Great, do you want to meet at the park? Is that far from you?"

"No. It's not far. I can do that."

"Great. Meet you in an hour?"

"Okay."

"Perfect," he says, and I can hear his smile. "Meet me at the pond, on the corner of fifth."

"Okay." I can't seem to form words, my mind still trying to process the fact that I am making plans to meet up with Charlie.

Charlie.

"Perfect. I'll see you in an hour." He sounds like a little kid on Christmas.

I take a shower after I hang up and blow-dry my hair. It's not something I do often because my hair is usually in a bun for work. It's also so long and thick it takes about a half-hour just to dry, but I need something to occupy my time for the next hour or I'll panic.

Literally.

Forty-five minutes later, hair curled and lipstick on with my favorite purple sweater, I leave my apartment and head toward the park. It's a quick walk, maybe ten minutes. It sounds like I have this luxurious apartment overlooking Central Park, but nothing's as glamorous as it seems. I live on the second floor and on the opposite side of the building. If you look out Dannie's bedroom window, all you see is the deli across the street.

The city is already bustling with morning joggers and weekend workers. The sound is soothing. I take a few deep breaths trying to calm my nerves when I spot his blonde curls.

They're messier today than they were the other night.

He hated his hair when I first met him. His mom tried to tame it when he was little, but quickly gave up. Those curls couldn't be tamed. He hated it so much in grade school because kids would make fun of him. I'm not really sure when he stopped caring. He stopped complaining about it in eighth grade. I don't know what changed, but one day we went to school, a kid came over and made a joke about his mop head, but Charlie didn't say a word. He just started talking to me about the donuts he'd brought me. He never complained about his hair again.

I always loved it. It was very out of character. Charlie was extremely structured and meticulous. You saw it in the way he lined his shoes up or the perfect notes he took in class or how he'd color-code his sheet music in band. Everything had its place, and everything was in its place. Nothing in his life was chaotic. Except his hair.

I remember how often I'd run my fingers through it, twisting curls around my index finger while we watched the sunset or drove around town just to drive after he got his license.

I find myself smiling as I come up behind him. He must hear me approach because he turns suddenly, and those grey eyes find mine instantly.

"You came," he smiles.

The constant surprise in his tone shouldn't hurt. I've been avoiding him for years, he has every reason to doubt me. But it still stings.

I offer him a small smile. "It's a beautiful morning."

He eyes trail down my body quickly before catching my eyes again. "Yeah, it is."

I can't help the blush that creeps up my neck. I'm probably reading way too much into the interaction, but I can't help it. I haven't been alone like this with a man in years.

Not that we're alone, necessarily. We have an entire city of people surrounding us. But when he looks at me like that it feels like we're the only two people in the world. Especially when he smiles like that.

His smile is wide, his mouth perfectly symmetrical. He never had braces, lucky him. His teeth were naturally straight except for one canine that stuck out slightly on the left. His lips were always on the larger side, but they seem bigger now, smiling at me.

Maybe I'd just forgotten what his smile looked like.

The thought makes my chest hurt.

"There is a little café that just opened a few blocks down, I figured we could walk," he says.

I nod. "Sure."

He gestures his head in the direction he wants to go and leads the way as I follow quietly beside him.

"So," he starts, running a hand through his hair making it look even more disheveled. "How are you?"

I almost laugh at the mundane question. I'm not sure what I expected. It's not like he's going to dump all of the hard questions right at the beginning, but I couldn't help but prepare for that on the short walk over here.

"I'm good. How about you?" I ask.

"Good, good. Busy."

"With work?"

He nods. "Yeah, Walt just opened his practice two years ago, so there's still a lot of growth happening. He's constantly bringing on new clients, but we don't really have the staff for it yet. Most days are about twelve hours."

"Wow. That sounds...exhausting." I couldn't imagine listening to people's problems for twelve hours straight. I can hardly listen to my own problems.

"It's not bad. I love my job."

"You do?" I say, unable to hide the surprise in my voice.

He laughs a little. "Are you surprised?"

"Well, yeah," I say honestly. "I guess I just never pictured you...sitting in an office all day."

"Honestly, I didn't either," he says as he takes a step closer to me to let other pedestrians pass. His cologne is subtle. It's the same one he was wearing at the restaurant. He smells different than I remember. He always smelled like summer to me. Maybe it's because we spent so much time at the lake. Now he smells like the city - fresh coffee and salty ocean air.

"Then what got you into it?" I ask and his face changes. His eyes catch mine and he stares for a moment before turning back toward our destination.

"Guess I just wanted to make a difference," he says it carefully and I wonder if there's more to it. But I don't feel like I'm in any position to push, so I let it go.

"Well, it's incredible. Surprising as it is, I'm sure you're amazing at it."

"Thanks." The corner of his mouth lifts in a smile. "What about you? I know where you work, but what else is going on in your life?"

"Not much, just work. Same as you, it keeps me pretty busy. Dannie and I spend a lot of time rehearsing,"

"Dannie is the pianist?" he asks.

I nod. "My roommate, too."

"Oh wow. Did you meet at work?"

"Yeah, she started a few weeks after I did."

"You've known her for a while, then?"

"Yeah, she's great. Her and Walker are pretty much my best friends."

"Walker?"

There is a slight hitch in his voice when he says Walker's name.

I nod. "He's the chef and part owner of *La Mer à Boire.*"

"Did you meet at work?" His eyebrows are close together and I can feel the unasked questions.

"Yes, I did. The three of us spend a lot of time together. Him and Dannie are...complicated, I'm pretty much the third wheel."

His face relaxes immediately, and I can't help the flutter that runs through my heart at the idea of him being jealous. It's unfair of me.

"How is your family?" he asks, changing the subject.

I realize suddenly I don't have much to say. I don't talk to my family enough. I could ask about his, but I also don't know if I want the answers. It's not that I don't care. I love his family. Charlie's parents were practically my parents and vice versa. Our families were extremely close. Our parents went on double dates together and his mom was the one who bought me my first box of tampons when I started my period at her house in eighth grade.

But I've spent so much time trying to forget everything and everyone in my past life in hopes of moving on – in hopes of letting *them* move on, I don't even know how to merge my old life with my new life. My therapist says I shouldn't do that. That the only way for me to really move forward is to accept my past and allow it to be a part of my future. Allow all the important people in my life back into my life.

But what does he know.

"Good," I say. "Sandra is getting married."

"Yeah, I heard. Kara is pretty excited."

"They still keep in touch?" I don't know why this surprises me. Kara and Sandra were as inseparable as me and Charlie, but in all the years since I left, she's never once mentioned Kara.

His eyes widen a bit in surprise before he looks down at the ground.

"What?"

"They live together."

I stop dead in my tracks.

Our sisters live together. My sister lives with Charlie's sister.

And I didn't know.

"I didn't know that," I whisper.

"I'm sure Sandra was just being...cautious."

"Yeah, everyone likes to walk on eggshells around me," I say snippily before I can catch myself. "I'm sorry, that wasn't fair."

"It doesn't have to be fair to be true."

"You sound like my therapist," I laugh once before I realize what I've just said and slap my mouth shut. I don't share with people that I'm in therapy. It's not that I'm embarrassed or ashamed. Most people should be in therapy. The problem is, people think your life is their business and once they know you go to therapy, they want to know why. And that's not information I give out easily. Heck, I never even told Dannie.

I can see the questions in his eyes, but he doesn't ask them, and I release a grateful breath.

He smiles at me and we keep walking.

It was true, though, he did sound like my therapist. It's still so surprising to me, that he went into psychology. But at the same time, it makes sense. Charlie was always my favorite person to talk to. He listened intently, he never interrupted, he was always tactful in the way he spoke, and he never gave bad advice.

"How long have they lived together?"

"On and off. They lived together the summers they were home from school. But officially, six years, I think. Maybe five? Kara moved back to Scottsdale after she graduated from NAU."

Six years. It shouldn't surprise me that there are so many parts of my sister's life I know nothing about. I rarely call her and when I do there's this awkwardness in the air we can't seem to move past. We lost our relationship the night I left without a word and didn't call home.

I don't have a right to be upset that she's moved on without me. I'm the one who put us in this situation, but pain is pain whether it's justified or not. Or so my therapist says.

"When did you come to New York?" I ask, desperate for a change of subject.

"After I graduated UCLA. I was home the summer after, but my parents were looking to sell the house and there wasn't much left in Arizona for me." I ignore the way his voice cracks slightly on the last half of his sentence and the way he glances at me before continuing. "Seemed like a good time to get out. So, I applied to NYU, got in, and that was it."

"How did you get the job with Dr. Jones?" I ask, kicking rocks with the toe of my shoes.

"He does a mentorship with NYU. He was my mentor during my masters and told me I had a job when I graduated. I started right after graduation."

"Which was when?"

"Last April."

"So, you've been here for five years?" I ask.

"Almost."

I look up to see him already watching me. Five years we were in the same city and never saw each other. What brought us together now?

"Can I ask you something?" I say, stopping to turn toward him.

"Anything," he says, his grey eyes searching mine and suddenly I feel claustrophobic. Like he can see every intimate thought and feeling when he looks at me so intently. I shift my gaze lower, just at the tip of his nose before I ask my next question.

"Did you go to school that fall?"

He thinks for a moment before responding. Probably trying to decide whether to tell me the truth or not.

"No," is all he says.

I don't know what answer I expected, but 'no' isn't the one I wanted. I left because I wanted *him* to leave. Because he needed to leave. To go to school and live his life. Without me getting in the way.

"I refused to leave," he starts. "I think your parents almost got a restraining order, to be honest," he laughs once, humorlessly. "I went over there almost every day asking for your new number. I didn't believe them when they said they didn't know it, I thought they were just trying to keep you from me. Your dad even called the cops on me one night after I spent an entire day sitting on your porch."

He shoves his hands in his pants pockets. "After that I called or texted Sandra multiple times to see if you'd called. I figured if anyone would tell me Sandra would. And she did. She called me a few months later to tell me she'd heard from you. That was when I realized they hadn't been lying and you'd really left without a word. It was the beginning of October."

"It was the first time I called home," I say quietly.

I remember that day. It was a warm, humid day in the city. Dannie and I had just moved in together and I hadn't spoken to my family in two months. I'd gone to a few therapy sessions and my therapist had recommended a couple support groups I could join. I was getting close with Dannie and even Walker. I had just started to feel like I was getting somewhere. My therapist was the one who suggested I call home.

"She wouldn't tell me where you were, I don't know why, but eventually, I stopped asking. She would text me sometimes though, just so I knew you were okay."

"I asked her not to," I say, unsure when I decided to be so truthful.

"What?" his eyebrows furrow and eyes scan my face.

"When I called Sandra that first night in October, she told me you'd asked about me. I asked her not to tell you where I was or give you my phone number."

He has his best poker face on. He's upset, but he's trying to hide it.

"I didn't know you were home, I figured you'd texted her or something. She never told me you stayed."

He doesn't say anything.

We stand in silence for a moment, listening to the sounds of the park before he speaks. "This is the café," he says, pointing behind me. "We should probably get in line, it can get busy quick."

"Look, I – " I start, but he cuts me off.

"It's okay, Penny, I get it." He's brushing it off, putting on a brave face for my benefit.

But I don't want a brave face. I want him to yell at me, blame me, leave me. Anything but understand me. He's always been so...perfect. Maybe too perfect.

There was always a part of me that wanted him to be upset with me. That wanted him to fall apart just like everyone else around me had. It made it easier for me to leave believing that one day he'd finally realize how difficult I'd made his life and he would get angry and forget me. Just once I want him to put all the blame where it belongs.

But here he is, all these years later, being the same incredibly patient, loving, supportive, empathetic person he's always been.

And I'm not sure I deserve it.

chapter thirteen

then

Graduation was looming. It was the one thing we never wanted to talk about.

I'd decided to stay in the valley and go to ASU for their music program. Mrs. Jensen had put in a good word with the department head and I was accepted into the program for Violin Performance. My audition had gone okay. I'm still convinced I only got in because she knew the dean. Charlie told me I was a shoo-in because I was the best violinist they'd ever heard. But he had to say that, he was my boyfriend. He just needed to guarantee kisses.

It took me weeks to tell him I'd been accepted. When I'd gotten my rejection letter from UCLA a few days before we'd both sat on his bed in silence, the truth hanging over us like a dark cloud.

There was no option for us to be together. He couldn't give up his dream for UCLA and he had received a call that a full-ride scholarship was in the works. Nothing had been confirmed, but the potential was there. He couldn't give it all up to go to ASU with me and I didn't get into UCLA.

We were stuck. Charlie was going to California. I was staying in Arizona. 397 miles would separate us for the next four years.

"It's going to be okay, Penny. I'll still come home for summers and holidays and we'll talk all the time." He kissed my tears away and rubbed my arm, but it couldn't fix the inevitable.

I knew he meant it, but I couldn't help but think that he'd go to school and realize there was so much more out there for him than me. It was the first time I really questioned whether our future together was guaranteed.

I smiled, kissed his cheek and we went on ignoring reality.

We practiced in my backyard, we planned our prom night and talked about how we were going to spend our last summer together with trips to the lake, walks at the park and movie nights in his room.

When the last week of school came, there was an unspoken sadness between us that we both tried to ignore. Charlie was quiet, which was so out of character. I didn't know what to say or do to fix it. I held his hand tighter as we walked home from school and played with his curls when he rested his head on my lap in my backyard. Neither of us were in the mood to practice anymore.

I went shopping with my mom for a prom dress at the last possible minute. There weren't a lot of options left, but there was a lavender dress that brushed the top of my knees with a glittery tulle skirt. It had a single strap over my right shoulder and made my chest look far more exciting than it was.

It was perfect.

Prom was the night before the last day of school. It was usually a few weeks before, but the prom committee had forgotten to schedule the catering and had to push it out to the end of the year. As I put on my makeup it hit me that tomorrow was the end. It was the last time I'd walk with Charlie to the bus stop or school. The last time we'd sit at our lunch table sharing donuts.

This was it.

"Charlie's here," I heard my mom shout from down the stairs as I applied the last bit of lipstick. It was sticky and felt thick on my lips. I never wore lipstick. I wore a bit of foundation and some mascara on my regular days. But today was prom. I'd borrowed some of Sandra's eyeshadow and lipstick for the night.

"Coming," I shouted down as I grabbed my clutch purse and checked myself one last time in my floor-length mirror.

I threw a lip-gloss into my purse and practically ran down the stairs to meet him. I came to an abrupt halt a few steps from the bottom when I caught sight of Charlie who was already looking at me.

His eyes were wide, his mouth slightly open. He was in a light-grey suit accentuating the grey of his eyes. He refused to rent a tux. Said it was a waste of money for one high school party. I'd originally argued, considering his parents would be paying and everyone rented a tux, but seeing him in his perfectly fitted suit, I couldn't remember why I'd wanted him in anything else.

He looked perfect and so much older. His face was freshly shaved, and his hair was brushed back as best as it could be, a few curls tickling the top of his ears. He hadn't had a haircut in a while, after I told him I preferred his hair longer.

"Penny," he breathed. "You're beautiful."

I smiled wide. "You should wear suits more often."

He laughed at that.

"I got this for you." He held a beautiful corsage out to me. It was a dark purple carnation and accented my dress perfectly.

"It's beautiful," I said as he took it out of the box and slid it onto my wrist.

"Only because it's on you."

I blushed before I reached into my purse. "I got you something, too."

I carefully pulled the tie out of my bag that I'd spent hours on the night before. I'd stayed awake until one in the morning trying to perfect it.

"I already have a tie," he said, lifting his to examine it. "Do you not like this one?"

"No, it's great, I just...here" I said, holding it out to him so the etching stood out. He took it carefully, tracing his fingers over the needlework at the end.

"It's kind of messy," I said. "I did it myself. I watched a video online. Surprisingly, the C was significantly harder than the P. I stuck my finger a million times." I lifted my band-aid clad thumb up to show him, but his eyes were still on the tie.

We stood there in silence for so long that I got nervous he didn't like it and was trying to find a nice way to say so.

"Your tie is nice though, you don't have to wear – "

"I love it, Penny," he finally said, meeting my eyes. His voice was deep. Almost rough. Looking back, I think he was trying not to cry, but at the time I never could've believed Charlie would cry over anything, much less a necktie.

"Really?"

He nodded.

"Will you wear it?" I asked.

"Of course," he said as he reached up and loosened the tie he was wearing. I stood in awe as he removed the knot from his neck and replaced it with mine. I never knew removing a necktie could be so...sensual, but I'm pretty sure I turned beet red watching him loosen one then tighten the other.

When the tie was finally in place, he took my hand and pulled me down the last few steps until our bodies met.

"I love you, Penny," his forehead fell to mine, his breath tickling my nose.

"I love you, Charlie."

"Alright, alright," my mom said, storming back into the entry. "We need a picture before you kids go."

Charlie squeezed my hand and kissed my cheek softly, before we were ushered into the living room to get every cliché prom picture known to man. After what felt like hours, we finally separated ourselves from our adoring mothers and made our way to Charlie's truck where he opened the door for me and helped me climb up.

We held hands over the center console the whole drive to the prom and he kept his arm around my waist as we entered the school gym. We took pictures under the archway and danced until our feet hurt. We tasted punch that was so terrible, we left our half full cups on a random table before making our way back to the dance floor.

"Promise me this is forever," he whispered against my cheek as we swayed in a slow circle.

"What?" I pulled back to catch his eye.

"Promise me when I go to school, nothing changes." His eyes held mine and I could see the fear behind them. The fear we'd both felt, but had ignored all these weeks.

"Charlie, I love you."

He dropped his forehead to mine. "Don't leave me."

How could I when he was the one leaving me?

I didn't say that though, I just held him as tight as I could.

Charlie's hands never left my body that night. Whether we were dancing or sitting at a table talking or chatting with our classmates, he was always touching me. His hand holding mine, his palm splayed on my lower back, his fingers grazing my waist.

He never let me go.

He kissed me on my front porch longer than normal. He told me he loved me a million times before he finally left me on the porch fighting tears. And as I lay in bed that night waiting for him to crawl through my window, I couldn't help but realize he never made me any promises that he would never leave *me.*

chapter fourteen

now

Three days. That's how long it takes for him to contact me after our breakfast.

After the awkward moment before we got in line at the cafe, things shifted to easy conversation. He asked about pieces I'd been working on, and I asked him about his family. His sister was teaching at our old middle school and his parents had moved to northern Arizona a few years previously.

The conversation had flowed easily. Easier than I thought it would.

It was like nothing had changed.

So why hasn't he called?

"He's going to call," Dannie says, coming into the kitchen Tuesday night.

"Who?" I ask, looking up from my phone.

She just rolls her eyes. "You know who. The one that's had you smiling more in the last three days than the eight years I've known you."

"I haven't been smiling more than usual."

"Yes, you have," Walker chimes in. "You actually went to karaoke with us last night. You almost gave me a heart attack when you agreed to go."

He's right. I never go to karaoke. Walker and Dannie go at least once a month on our nights off. It's the only time they're remotely civil with each other. A mutual love for karaoke can bring anyone together. At least, that's what Walker tells me.

They've asked me a few times to go, and I always say no. I hate the crowd, the drinking, the loud music. Last night they asked if I wanted to go to a new karaoke place they'd found. It was farther upstate, and the best part was it wasn't a bar. It was just a small coffee shop that stays open late Monday nights specifically for karaoke. Shocking them and myself, I'd said yes.

I'd actually had fun. I only lasted an hour, watching, keeping myself away from the stage, before I told them I was going to catch an early train home. I couldn't wait to tell my therapist. This was more than starting small.

I'd say it was at least medium.

"I wondered if it was about a guy." Walker continues. He tosses a towel over his shoulder and leans against the counter, arms crossed. "So, who is he?"

"The guy that chased her through the kitchen the other night," Dannie answers, taking a seat next to me, her hand automatically falling to her stomach.

"You mean the one that made me drop my soufflé?"

"Yes, but I'm sure that could only improve it," Dannie says.

Walker laughs but doesn't respond to her. "So, what's the story? Old boyfriend?"

I nod.

"Have you seen him since?" he asks.

"We went to breakfast on Saturday."

"And she's totally in love with him," Dannie says.

"I'm not..." I start, but I'm not sure how to finish that sentence.

Dannie just raises her eyebrows.

Of course, I love Charlie. I always will. He was my best friend for almost ten years of my life. I couldn't *not* love him. But that didn't mean I was still *in* love with him. I hadn't seen him in years.

"I haven't seen him since I was eighteen," I say. "We don't even know each other anymore."

"People don't change that much, Penny," Walker says.

"Walker's right," Dannie starts, but is interrupted by a look of shock on Walker's face. "What?"

"I'm sorry," he says, slapping a hand on his chest in mock surprise, "did Dannielle Lynn Brookes just utter the words 'Walker's right'?"

She gives him her most unimpressed look. "Don't get used to it."

"I think we might have to check the temperature in hell, Penny," he jokes.

"Am I paying you all to gossip like teenagers?" Jade asks, storming into the kitchen.

"Of course not, you're paying us to suffocate under the pressure of misogyny and stolen money," Dannie deadpans.

"Dannielle," Jade starts with a sigh, her fingers going to the bridge of her nose. "What would you do if your precious, innocent child spoke like that?"

Dannie just shrugs one shoulder. "Give him a high five and buy him some ice cream."

Jade takes a breath like she's going to fight back, but Walker jumps in. "Alright ladies, we have a full dining room out there that I'm sure is waiting on dessert and beautiful music. We best get back to work."

Jade eyes Dannie for another beat then sticks her nose in the air with a little "humph" as she walks out the swinging door.

Dannie turns to Walker. "How do you know her again?"

"She was married to my cousin for a few years," he shrugs.

"Someone married that?"

He laughs and I grab Dannie's arm to pull her back into the dining room.

It's a quiet night. Tuesdays are usually busier than this, people trying to get through the work week after surviving a Monday, but there are at least a dozen empty tables which has Jade in a complete frenzy for the rest of the night. She makes her rounds, schmoozing the crowd while Dannie and I play the same five songs we've been playing for months.

I wanted to pick out a few new pieces, but ever since Dannie found out she was pregnant she's been particularly feisty and refuses to learn anything new, so we've stuck to the basics. By the time the night is done, my feet are tired, Dannie's on the verge of plucking out Jade's eyebrows and Walker's spent the last hour cornering Dannie in the kitchen to prevent aforementioned eyebrow plucking while I played the last set.

It's one in the morning by the time we all leave. Dannie and I sometimes stay late to help Walker clean the kitchen. His two employees quit a few weeks into the new year and he hasn't been able to find any replacements. Dannie moans and groans about staying late, but I know she likes it. She hates walking home alone, whether she will admit it or not, and especially since she got pregnant.

"Are we even on your way home, or do you just enjoy stalking us?" Dannie asks Walker, her sour mood getting worse by the second.

"You know where I live, Dannie, you've been to my apartment a million times," Walker says. "And if I recall, you were the one that asked me to walk you home."

"I didn't ask, I simply said it wasn't safe for two beautiful young women to walk the streets of New York City alone after midnight."

Walker just smiles as he shuts off the last light in the kitchen. Her snide remarks never earn her the response she wants from him. He usually laughs or smiles, he never gets angry or impatient with her.

"Oh, Penny, I almost forget. Someone dropped something off for you earlier," he says, turning back into the kitchen.

"What?"

"Here," he says, coming back through the swinging doors with a small gold box and a logo I don't recognize.

"Oh, *Dana's Bakery*! They have the best donuts," Dannie says.

"Who's it from?" I ask Walker.

"Not sure. The company's delivery driver dropped it off. Is there no card?"

I shake my head.

"Well, open it!" Dannie says impatiently.

I lift the lid carefully to find a half dozen powdered donuts perfectly lined side by side with a handwritten note scrawled on the inside of the lid.

I hope these are still your favorite. Dinner tomorrow?

"Oh," Dannie croons. "Is this from lover boy?"

I'd roll my eyes if I wasn't smiling. I close the lid and clear my throat. "It's getting late, we should probably head out."

"You should call him," Dannie starts as Walker locks the front door behind us.

"It's one in the morning."

"Okay, then text him."

"Now?"

"Yes, Penny, now. You're not getting any younger here."

I look to Walker for advice, but he just offers me a comforting smile.

"I'll text him when I get home," I say, suddenly nervous.

"No, text him now. We're not leaving until you do," she says firmly, crossing her arms over her chest.

"Dannie, it's freezing, let's go," I say pulling her arm, but she doesn't budge.

"What are you so afraid of, Penny?" she asks, softer this time.

I look down at the box of donuts and think back to the last time I saw Charlie all those years ago. All the crying, screaming, fighting...painful memories. I think about why I left in the first place. I left for a reason, a *good* reason. And I haven't gone back for better ones.

Yes, we had fun at breakfast. Yes, the conversation flowed easily. But we didn't talk about anything important. We talked about music and our families. We talked about our coworkers and our favorite places to eat in the city. We never talked about *us*.

I look back up at Dannie, her eyebrows raised in question.

"Everything," I whisper.

Her eyes soften and I see Walker lift his hand like he's going to rub my arm or back to comfort me before he catches himself and puts his hand in his jacket pocket, which just makes me even more afraid.

How am I supposed to see Charlie again when I can't even handle Walker touching me. Walker who has been one of the steadiest people in my life in the last eight and a half years. Who has walked me home almost every single night after work because he wants to make sure I get home okay. Who plays mine and Dannie's favorite pop songs while we clean the kitchen even though he hates them. Who can't even rub my arm in comfort because he's afraid I'll have a panic attack.

"It's going to be okay, Penny," Dannie says, hooking her arm through mine, pulling me in the direction of our apartment.

We walk in silence the whole way home, Walker trailing behind us.

"Text me when you get inside," Walker says when we reach the front of our building.

"Thanks Walker," I say, "for everything."

"Anything for you, Penny," he says with a soft smile. "Goodnight, Dannie Lynn."

She doesn't acknowledge him, and he turns, heading farther down the street toward his apartment.

"Wait," she says to me as I reach for the door.

"What?"

"Look, I can't even begin to understand what you've gone through and I'm not going to pretend that I do. But..." she trails off, trying to find her words. "Don't give up on something good just because you're afraid." She looks back toward the direction Walker went. "Sometimes the greatest things in life are the most terrifying."

I'm not sure we're just talking about me anymore.

She turns back to me and if I didn't know better, I'd think there were tears pooling in her eyes. But Dannie doesn't cry.

"Is this advice for me or for you?"

She laughs, humorlessly. "Definitely you. I give advice, I don't take it. Now, let's get inside before my baby freezes and I give birth to Frosty."

And just like that Dannie's back. Her flippant, I-don't-care-about-anything attitude is sitting pretty while her true feelings are shoved to the back.

We climb the stairs to the second floor silently and she doesn't say a word until I unlock the door.

"Will you text Walker and let him know we're inside, I'm tired." She doesn't even glance my way before she closes the door to her bedroom.

I send Walker a quick text before brushing my teeth and pulling out the couch and it doesn't take long for my mind to wander and sleep to be impossible.

Leaving Scottsdale, leaving Charlie, was one of the hardest things I've ever done in my life. It wasn't a decision I made lightly and it's a decision I've stood by. When he mentioned how hard he'd tried to get in contact with me, I wasn't surprised. Sandra tried to get me to call him multiple times. She used to text me his number frequently, but I couldn't do it.

I saved his number in my phone at one point. I used to stare at it at night, my thumb hovering over the number willing myself to call him, but I couldn't make myself do it. Eventually, I deleted his number and Sandra stopped bringing him up.

Laying here now, his phone number glaring off my phone screen and my thumb hovering over it again, I can't make myself delete it. Not with his voice, his smile, his smell still fresh in my mind.

I take a deep breath and send him a text before I lose the nerve.

Me: Thanks for the donuts. They are, in fact, still my favorite.

I lock my phone and turn off the lamp hoping I will be able to get a few hours at, the least, but before my head even falls back onto the pillow, my phone lights up.

Charlie: I'm glad you liked them. I was nervous you grew into some donut aversion. Or worse, you became

one of those health nuts you see all over social media who only eat kale and spinach.

Me: No kale for me! Though I do enjoy spinach here and there.

Charlie: Please tell me it's on pizza or something and you don't just eat dry spinach on a salad?

Me: ...

Charlie: That's not the Penny I remember.

I have zero interest in talking about past anything. Especially over text message.

Me: Why are you awake at 1am?

Charlie: Went out with some friends.

Me: Don't you have to work early in the morning?

Charlie: No, I don't work on Wednesdays.

Me: Why not?

Charlie: I work on Saturday afternoons and late on Fridays. Wednesday is my weekend.

Charlie: Speaking of dinner...

Me: Were we talking about dinner?

Charlie: I thought it was a nice segue.

Me: I remember you being a better communicator.

Charlie: Sorry, I'm out of practice on this whole dating thing.

Dating thing? Was he trying to date me?

Charlie: I was thinking tomorrow?

Me: I have to be at work at six tomorrow.

Charlie: I can do an early dinner. 4?

I type a message before I delete it and try again. I wonder if he's sitting on his own bed watching the three dots appear and disappear.

Me: Sure. Where do you want to meet?

Charlie: I was thinking I could cook for you.

Charlie: At my place.

His place. Alone. Just the two of us.

For a moment, I forgot that we were practically strangers. With just a few text messages it's like nothing's changed. It's just me and Charlie again. Charlie and me. It's thrilling and scary at the same time how quickly we can fall into a pattern we haven't traced in almost a decade. But then he throws a curveball and I'm thrust back into reality.

Charlie: If you're uncomfortable, we can meet somewhere, Penny.

Me: No.

Me: Dinner at your place sounds great.

Charlie: Are you sure?

Not even a little, I think.

Me: Yes.

Charlie: Then I'll see you at four.

Charlie: Goodnight Penny.

He sends me his address and I put my phone back on my nightstand.

Am I nervous? Yes.

Am I excited? Yes.

Do I sleep better than I have in years?

Yes.

chapter fifteen

then

"You know, you should really lock your door, if you're going to have boys over," Sandra's voice was loud, too loud. Did she want to wake the whole house? She shut the door behind her, one eye on Charlie.

"Hello Sandra, always a pleasure," he said, with a cocky grin.

"Get out, I need to talk to my sister. And my parents are still awake. Be more careful next time," she said, plopping herself on the edge of my bed.

"Sandra, it's almost one in the morning," I said with a groan.

"Exactly, so lover boy should be long gone by now." She winked at him, and I rolled my eyes. "It is a school night after all."

"It's the last day of senior year, it's not like anything important is happening tomorrow," I argued.

"It's okay, I can take a hint," Charlie said, grabbing his shirt off my desk chair and sliding it over his head. "I'll see you tomorrow."

He kissed my lips quickly before sneaking out my window. He was a pro at that point. I didn't even hear the back gate close.

"What do you want?" I asked, falling back onto my pillow regretting flying her home early from school to make it to my graduation.

Sandra shifted until her head was next to mine. "Are you guys having sex?"

"What?" I yelled as loud as I could in a whisper, turning to face her. "Did you really wake me up at one o'clock in the morning to ask me if I'm...doing that?"

"Well, no, but I got sidetracked. He's here almost every night and I'm supposed to believe you two are just *sleeping*?" She raised her eyebrow at me.

She was the first to discover Charlie had been spending the night. It was a few weeks into junior year when Charlie started sneaking into my room at night. It wasn't every night, maybe once or twice a month, but Sandra ran into him one morning when he was sneaking out. She'd given me a side-eye glance, rolled her eyes and never said another word about it. We lasted a whole year before my mom found out. It was that summer before senior year started. We were still at the lake house and Charlie had woken up too late. My mom had come in to get the laundry and found him in my bed. He'd bolted out of bed with a bright red face and offered a kind "good morning," before heading back to his room. My mom had left without a word. It took a few hours before I found the courage to leave my room and face her. She was quiet as I came downstairs.

As I stood next to the kitchen island, she grabbed a box of condoms out of her purse and said, "Don't give your body to someone you can't give your heart to."

It was the greatest advice she could've given me. She never brought it up again. I think she thought once we got home, we would go back to our respective bedrooms at night, but there was no way that was going to happen after we had the whole summer sharing a bed every single night. I never slept well the few nights he did stay home.

I rolled my head to look at Sandra and asked, "Are you having sex with Jared?"

"Jeremy. And no, we broke up." She tried to say it nonchalantly, but I could tell something was wrong.

"What? When?" I asked, propping myself up on my arm.

She raised her arm, tapping at the imaginary watch on her wrist. "Thirty minutes ago."

"Why?"

We all loved Jeremy. Okay, maybe loved is a strong word, I couldn't even remember his name. But he was the best Sandra had ever brought home. She dated the worst guys in high school. She'd met Jeremy right before she left for UCLA. They decided to try long distance, much to our parents' dismay, and Sandra had said everything was going well. She had been excited to come home for the summer holiday and see him.

"Long distance," she shrugged. "We rarely see each other with me in California."

"I guess that makes sense," I said.

"But don't worry, I'm sure you and Charlie will be just fine."

"What does this have to do with Charlie?" I asked, eyebrows tight together.

She turned her head to look at me. "I mean, he wants to go to UCLA, too, right?"

I nodded. "He's waiting to hear about a scholarship. I'm sure he got it, though."

"Yeah, cause he's like, weirdly smart."

I didn't respond, thinking about what she'd said. I hadn't let myself think about it much. We both knew what was coming, but we hadn't brought it up since I got my acceptance letter to ASU. We still talked about the future all the time like how many kids we wanted or where we wanted to vacation when we were old, but not real-life. It was always about our daydream future.

"Like I said," she said, pulling me from my thoughts. "You guys will be fine." She waggles her eyebrows at me. "Especially if you're having sex. Phone sex, am I right?"

"Oh my gosh, Sandra, don't be gross," I groaned as I threw a pillow at her head.

"So...are you?"

"Am I what?"

She rolled her eyes. "You know what."

"No," I said, laying back down on my pillow. "We aren't."

"Really?" she asked doubtfully.

"What?"

"I'm just surprised. I figured you guys had done it long ago. I mean you've known each other forever and you do sleep in the same bed almost every night."

"Why the sudden interest in my sex life?"

She sighed and closed her eyes, "I didn't break up with Jeremy, he...cheated on me. He's been sleeping with some chick he works with."

"Oh my gosh, Sandra, I'm so sorry."

She wiped a tear off her cheek that I'm sure fell without her permission. Sandra's never been a crier. "It's whatever. There are a lot of good guys at school that I haven't gone out with because Jeremy was here. Now I'm not tied down to anyone."

"Had you guys...?"

"No. He said that was the problem. He needed a girl who could be in a grown-up relationship," her fingers formed air quotes around 'grown-up'.

"I'm sorry." I said again, not sure what else to say. Sandra's only eighteen months older than me, but it always felt like a bigger gap. Maybe it's because she had such a strong personality and was so unafraid. I felt like she had experienced so much in life I hadn't yet. I never really thought about it, but I figured she'd slept with at least one of her boyfriends by now.

"It's just...sex is a big deal. I don't want to just give it to anyone."

"You don't have to."

"It's like mom always says, 'don't give your body to someone' – "

"'You can't give your heart to'," I finished.

"Yeah. I think that's really good advice."

"It is."

She turned her head again to look at me. "Do you love Charlie?"

"Of course I do," I said, quickly.

"No, like really love him. I mean, could you see yourself sleeping with him? I mean...*sleeping* with him."

I thought about it for a moment before I answered. It was something I'd thought about before, more than once. Usually when I was with Charlie in the bed of his truck or my bed when his hands and lips were on me, and I never wanted him to leave. But I'd never thought about it when I was alone with a clear head.

But the answer was so obvious.

I nodded. "Yeah. I do."

"See, that's what I want. I want to sleep with someone I love."

"There's nothing wrong with waiting, Sandra."

"I know," she sighed, wiping more tears off her cheeks.

I grabbed her arm closest to me and wrapped my arms around it giving her the best hug I could laying down.

"Thanks, Penny," she said, and I felt her head fall on top of mine.

"For what?"

"Listening."

"Anytime."

We fell asleep like that.

chapter sixteen

now

"Penny?" Sandra picks up with urgency.

"Why is it every time I call, you answer the phone like you already know someone's died?" I ask putting the phone on speaker so I can finish my makeup.

"You don't call that often, it's more likely you're calling because someone *has* died," she says it sarcastically, but there is a bite behind her words. Sandra's never been one for subtlety.

"Sorry."

She sighs. "No, I'm sorry. Just stressed with all the wedding planning."

"That crazy, huh?" I say as I apply my eyeshadow.

"You have no idea. I told mom we wanted a small, intimate wedding and I think she invited the entire Phoenix population."

I chuckle. "She does love parties."

My mother has thrown the most outrageous parties in her lifetime. She was always a little disappointed whenever my birthday came around and all I wanted was family-only with pizza and games. She was ecstatic when I started inviting the Wrights. It may have been small, but it was still a party. And no one threw a party like Kathy Maine.

"Have you found your dress yet?" I ask.

"Not yet. I'm going shopping next week."

"Is mom going with you?"

"Not sure, she might have to work."

I suddenly feel even more guilty. If I was there, I'd go with her. I *should* go with her to get her dress. That's an important day. "You're going alone?"

"No, uh, my maid of honor is going with me."

"Who is your maid of honor?"

"Kara." She says it so quietly and quickly the only reason I hear it is because I already guessed the answer.

"You can talk about them, Sandra, it's been eight years, I'm not going to break just by the mere mention of them."

"No one thinks you're going to break, Penny."

"Then how come you never told me you lived with her?" I blurt out before I can stop myself.

I can almost hear her eyes widen. "Penny, none of us knew how to handle it, we just wanted – wait. How did you know I live with Kara?"

Dang it. I didn't think this through.

"Mom told me," I lie quickly.

"I just talked to mom this morning and she said she hadn't heard from you since you cut her off on your birthday. Which, by the way, you need to call and apologize for."

"I had something come up. I told her I would call her later."

"What came up?"

"I ran into someone at the restaurant," I say, trying to be as vague as possible. "I wanted to say hi before they left."

"You have no friends, Penny."

"Wow, thanks."

"Sorry, but it's true. You don't talk about anyone but Dannie and Walker and both of them work with you. So, you're going to have to come up with a better lie."

"You were the one lying about Kara for the last how many years again? Shouldn't I be yelling at you, not the other way around."

"I'm not yelling, I'm speaking sternly," she says. "Besides, I wasn't lying. I just wasn't sharing. I'm not obligated to share every single detail of my life with you. Lord knows you don't share ninety percent of your life with us."

I don't respond, unsure how to fight back when everything she's said is right. I haven't shared my life with them. I have ignored many phone calls and text messages over the years. I have no right to be angry with how they've dealt with that.

"So, how did you know?" she presses.

I take a deep breath and close my eyes tightly. "I ran into her brother."

The silence is deafening.

Eventually, I break it and ask, "Are you still there?"

"You ran into Charlie?" she yells and I drop my mascara tube in the sink.

"Yes."

"At the restaurant?"

"Yes."

"Did he know you worked there?"

"No."

"Woah. I mean, I knew he was in New York, but it's a big city. I never thought you'd run into him."

It takes me a minute to register what she's said.

"Wait, you knew he was in the city?"

"Of course, I knew. I live with his sister. And he calls me sometimes. He's my friend, too."

She's right. Charlie was never just mine. Sandra spent the summers at the lake house, too. She was at our family game nights and dinners. He was her family as much as he was mine.

"Are you okay?" she asks, much softer this time.

"Yeah. I mean, it was a total shock. I think I was speechless for a solid two minutes, but...it was nice to see him."

"It was?" Disbelief coats her words.

"Yes."

"Are you going to see him again?"

"Yeah, he invited me to dinner tonight."

"And you're going?" She sounds unsure.

"Yes. Should I not?"

"No! Of course, you should go. I'm just surprised you said yes."

"Well, I did. I'm getting ready. I leave in an hour."

"I'm really happy for you, Penny."

"This doesn't mean anything. It's just dinner with an old friend." The last thing I need is her getting her hopes up. Or worse, getting mine up.

"No, it's dinner with Charlie and that's a big deal. Don't pretend it's not."

"It doesn't have to be a big deal."

"Do you remember when you called me the first time after you left? Do you remember what you said when I asked why you left?"

It takes me a minute to remember the conversation. I sigh. "Yes."

She doesn't respond and I know she's waiting for me to remind her and myself.

"I left because I didn't want him to give anything up for me," I whisper.

"And you remember what I said?" She doesn't wait for me to respond. "That it's his decision to make, not yours."

I put my mascara back in my makeup bag and look at myself in the mirror. I look older. I've grown out my hair, it almost reaches the top of my jeans, and my skin's clearer from the humidity, but I still see the same naïve, eighteen-year-old girl that came to New York with a backpack and tears. That same girl who hid away from everything and everyone. Who doesn't know how to fight back when life throws punches.

"Sandra – "

"No, Penny. Don't make the same mistakes twice. Don't run away from him."

"Why are you so sure I'll run?"

"Because he loved you. Even after everything that happened, he loved you. And I think that scared you more than anything else that happened that summer."

chapter seventeen

then

"Bird!" Sandra yelled. "No, plane! Surfboard! Green beans!"

"Okay, now you're just shouting random words," I said, hands on my hips.

"No talking," Charlie said.

I glared at him, but he just grinned.

I sighed aggressively, then did the same move again with my arms out to the side.

"Time's up," my dad said holding the timer up high, like I couldn't see it.

"Skydiving," I snapped, sitting between my mom and Sandra.

"You did good, sweetie," Mrs. Wright said patting my knee.

"This isn't fair," Sandra said. "I never even wanted Penny on my team in the first place."

"Hey," I whined.

"I'm sorry Penny, but charades isn't exactly your forte."

"You guys were the ones that wanted boys versus girls," Charlie said, picking out his own card. "I'm sorry, *ladies.*"

"Misogyny doesn't look good on you," Kara said chucking a pillow at him.

"Good looks or not," he chucked the pillow right back at her. "We're still winning."

"That's right," my dad said, clapping his hands together. "Come on, son, show them what you've got!"

The game went on for another thirty minutes and somehow my dad and Charlie beat the girls. Five against two and we still lost - six to one. It was pathetic. We usually played against families, the Wright's versus the Maines, but Charlie's dad was away on business and Kara was in a mood and wanted to mix it up. Sandra thought it was a great idea and neither of the moms were listening when we picked teams, so I got outvoted.

We'd gathered together to celebrate mine and Charlie's last day of school. We'd screamed and yelled and jumped for joy when the last bell rang that afternoon and my parents had invited the Wright's over for a game night.

I felt Charlie before I saw him, a light touch on my waist, his breath on my ear.

"Take a walk with me."

I smiled as a shiver ran down my spine and nodded. He grabbed my hand and led me out the front door.

We walked in silence for a few minutes, hand in hand.

I loved the silence. Sandra thought it was weird. She'd come home from school and find me cleaning the kitchen in a quiet house and would immediately turn on the TV or radio in the background. I didn't mind the background noise, but I preferred the silence.

Silence held opportunity. It was a time to let my mind wander. To dream up every fantasy or stress over every unknown. Time to think about what I wanted or reminisce on the past. I was never afraid of my thoughts, good or bad.

Once Charlie came into my life, I spent a lot of my quiet time thinking about him. About his fingers brushing my neck or his shoulders hunched over a textbook. The look of concentration on his face when he played the saxophone or the sound of his laugh.

At that moment, walking down our street in silence all I could think about was my conversation with Sandra the night before.

"Have you heard back from UCLA?" I finally asked, breaking the silence.

I couldn't pinpoint the look that crossed his face – concern, confusion, fear? But he kept his eyes looking forward, away from me. "Yes," he finally said.

"And?"

He looked at me then, just out of the corner of his eye. "Full-ride."

"Charlie!" I squealed, throwing my arms around his neck. "I'm so proud of you! When did you hear?"

"A few days ago," he said into my neck.

I pulled back a few inches to look at him. "Why didn't you tell me?"

"It's not a big deal," he said with a light shake of his head.

"Not a big deal? Charlie, you've been dreaming of UCLA like, forever. Of course it's a big deal."

He just shrugged and started walking again.

I hated it when he shrugged. "What is it?"

"I don't know if I want to go."

"What?" I shouted. I tugged his arm, pulling him to a stop to face me. "You already accepted."

"I know, but I could still change my mind."

"Charlie, why in the world would you change your mind? It's a full-ride – "

"Penny," he said grabbing my waist and pulling me to him. "Can we not talk about this? I don't want to think about school. It's a beautiful night and I just want to take a quiet walk with my even more beautiful girlfriend."

I didn't want to stop talking about it. I wanted to understand more. I wanted to ask more questions. I should have asked more questions. But Charlie rarely avoided topics of conversation, which meant this was important to him. So, I let it go. We could talk about it later.

He kissed my forehead, before taking my hand and continuing down the street.

"Did you get your cap and gown?" he asked.

"Yeah, my mom picked it up the other day. It's awful."

He laughed. "It is. I don't know who decided our school colors needed to be burnt orange.

"It's supposed to be the same color as the Arizona sun."

"It's hideous."

"Oh," I said, grabbing onto his arm with my free hand, "Did you hear Brandon Lee's having a graduation party?"

"Yeah."

"We should go."

He scoffed. "Why?"

"Because we only graduate high school once. It could be fun."

"I don't think that's a good idea," he said, shaking his head.

"Why not?"

"Because nothing good ever happens at those parties. There's always too much drinking and the cops always get called. Brandon's little brother got eight months of community service last time for streaking down the street."

"Well, unless you plan on taking off all your clothes in the street at some point in the night, I don't think we need to worry about that," I joked, but he didn't laugh.

"Why do you want to go?"

It was my turn to shrug. "I just thought it would be fun."

He stopped on the corner and stared at me for the longest time before finally responding. "Maybe."

"Maybe?"

"Maybe."

"I don't like that answer," I said, crossing my arms over my chest.

He grinned. "Then ask me better questions."

"Hm." I lifted my finger to my chin like I was contemplating. He took a step closer, hooking his finger around the one on my chin, tugging me toward him.

"Ask me a better question, Penny," he said again, his voice low. His rainy eyes focused only on me.

"If I kiss you, will you kiss me back?" I asked, repeating the same words he said to me that first time on my porch.

His grin widened. "Most definitely."

"Promise?" I said, wrapping my arms around his neck.

"Promise." He leaned closer.

So, I closed the distance between us, and he kept his promise.

chapter eighteen

now

I stand outside his front door for ten minutes.

The guy who lives next door has come and gone from his front door three times in the time I've been standing on his welcome mat like an idiot and I'm pretty sure he's about to call the cops on me.

Yes, I recognize that I am a coward, but here we are.

I take a deep breath, then three more, before I think back to Sandra telling me not to run. With her voice in my head, I lift my fist to the door and knock.

I'm not sure what I expect, but Charlie in a t-shirt and jeans with an apron tied around his waist is not it. My eyes bug out of my head, and he grins wide.

"Hi," he says.

"Hi," I say, taking another full body sweep at the apron-clad Charlie. His t-shirt is tight around his arms and his jeans hug his legs perfectly. Charlie was always on the skinnier side in high school, but he's filled out over the years going from boy to man. He ran a lot in high school, I wouldn't be surprised if he added weightlifting to his routine.

Elementary school Charlie was adorable. Middle school Charlie was cute. High-school Charlie was beautiful. But fully grown, manly Charlie is dead sexy.

"Come in." He steps to the side, allowing me access.

I take a step inside and immediately take off my shoes, lining them next to his by the front door. When I'm upright again and turn to face him, his grin has somehow widened.

"What?" I ask.

"You don't have to do that."

"Do what?"

He points to the floor. "Line up your shoes like that."

My mouth opens in shock. "If I recall, you were the one who told me I couldn't haphazardly toss my shoes around."

"I don't think I used the word haphazardly."

"You most definitely did. We were ten. You were the only ten-year-old using words like haphazardly. I had to look it up when I got home. I'd never even used a dictionary before."

He laughs once, then guides me toward the living room.

"There's not much to tour, but I'd be happy to give you one."

"I'd like that."

The space is not small, but also not large. The prefect size for one person. The entry opens to a decent-sized living room with a dining table off to the right side and the kitchen across from it. He has two big windows on the wall directly across from the front door overlooking the city. There is a huge flat screen TV on the wall to the left with a full-size, navy-blue couch and a single white chair facing it. It's beautiful and perfectly put together.

He takes me into the kitchen next. It's extremely small as most kitchens in the city are. It's bigger than mine and Dannie's, but not by much.

"It smells amazing. What are you making?" I ask, admiring the grey and blue backsplash.

"Pizza. With spinach, of course," he smirks.

"I figured the spinach was for the starter salad," I joke.

He just shakes his head at me. "Penny, Penny, Penny. At least you still like donuts, otherwise I might have an actual heart attack."

I smile. "I ate every single one."

"You already ate them all?" his eyes widen in surprise before he grins. "Guess some things never change."

My smile fades instantly. Things do change. Everything's changed.

I clear my throat. "Is it a two bedroom or one?"

"Two. I use the second as an office," he says, leading the way through the kitchen back past the living room and into the second room. There are two doors cornering each other next to the TV in the living room, one is closed, the other isn't. He flicks the light on in the room with the open door and I follow him in slowly. It's just as neat and tidy as the rest of the apartment. It's small and he hasn't filled it much. There is a desk in the center of the room on a rug and a single bookshelf to the left of it. My eyes scan the room quickly before they stop dead on a jar sitting on the corner of his desk. More specifically, the jar on the desk.

Full of pennies.

"What's this?" I ask, pointing to the jar.

"Oh, uh," he stammers. "It's nothing."

I look back at him still standing in the doorway, rubbing the back of his neck. The familiar tick hits me instantly and suddenly, he's fifteen again, rubbing his neck as he stares down at a problem he couldn't solve. Or rubbing his neck trying to think of a nice way to turn down Susie Winters for junior prom, or when he'd spent hours playing his saxophone and still didn't have the parts down.

He's uncomfortable and I want to know why.

"It's not nothing, you're rubbing your neck."

He drops his hand immediately and looks at me. I don't know if it's the instant familiarity that's getting to him or just his not wanting to respond, but he looks...shy. I have rarely ever seen Charlie shy, but it's the only word to describe the look on his face right now.

Minutes feel like hours before he finally says, "They're lucky pennies."

Oh. *Oh.*

Suddenly I remember a particular July 4th at the lake. My patriotic sundress and kisses in his truck.

"When did you start collecting them," I ask, tentatively.

His eyes never leave mine. "The day you left."

The words sting. Though, I don't think that was his intention.

"I stopped, though," he adds quickly.

"You stopped what? Collecting them?"

He nods.

"Why? When?"

"The day I saw you at *La Mer à Boire.*"

"Why?" I ask quietly.

He takes a deep breath before he responds. "Guess I didn't feel like I needed them anymore."

I'm not sure what to say to that. We stare at each other for a moment, his forehead furrowed, waiting for my reaction. I count to three in my head, take three deep breaths, before I reach into my purse and pull out my wallet. He watches me carefully as I open the zipper and remove the only coin in it.

The penny is shiny. I cleaned it that day after I got home then slipped it back in my wallet. I never took it out again. It looks brand new. I twist it between my fingers a couple times before I gently place it on top of his jar.

"Is that...?"

I nod. "Your first lucky penny."

His smile grows wide, all shyness gone, and he crosses his arms across his chest.

"You don't need it anymore?" He smiles cockily and I can't help the goosebumps that raise on my arm and the butterflies in my stomach.

He's flirting with me.

I shrug one shoulder, leaning against his desk and crossing my own arms, mimicking his stance.

"Not if you're here," I say, surprising myself with my forwardness. My eyes go wide when I realize what I've said, but he doesn't care. I catch the glimmer in his eyes, telling me he likes the flirting and suddenly there is a tension in the air that wasn't there before. A tension I haven't felt with a man in years. A tension that has him taking two, slow, tentative steps toward me, carefully watching for any indication that I want him to stop.

But for some irresponsible, reckless reason, I don't want him to stop.

He takes one more step until he's close enough that if I reached my hand out it would touch his chest.

"Charlie..." I say quietly and he jerks to a stop.

"You said my name." An unreadable expression crosses his face, his features going soft.

"Yes?" It comes out like a question because I'm not sure why he's looking at me like that.

"I missed that."

"What?"

"You," he says, taking another step closer. "Saying my name."

It's not until he points it out that I realize I haven't said his name. Not since he showed up at the restaurant. I didn't say it when he called me or took me to breakfast or even when we were texting. I haven't said it once. I think there was a part of me that was scared to acknowledge that he was really here. Like saying his name made it all more real. Made *him* more real. So instead, I just avoided it. Waiting for the moment we both realized too much had changed.

"Say it again," he says softly. "Please."

He's so close to me, I can feel his breath brushing lightly over my face. No part of his body is touching mine, but if I took the smallest step forward every single part of me would be touching him.

The timer on the oven beeps loudly, startling us both, and I practically jump onto the desk behind me.

"Pizza is done," he mumbles, but he doesn't move.

I smile and take a small step to the side and around him. Away from him. "We should eat then."

He notices the shift of direction, me literally pulling myself away from him, but he doesn't say anything. He just leads me to the kitchen and pulls out a perfectly cooked homemade pizza.

I don't even know how we got where we did in his office, but I also shouldn't be surprised. It's always been so easy with Charlie; I don't know why it surprises me that it still is. His grey eyes, cocky smile and flirty remarks take me right back to what we were and it's like the last eight years never happened.

But they did happen.

And we can't pretend they didn't.

"That was delicious. Where did you learn to cook like that?" I ask, pushing the empty plate away from me.

"Google," he laughs. "I was getting sick of ramen and fast food, so I figured I better learn how to cook. My mom may have given me a few lessons over video calls, as well."

"It was incredible, thank you."

We sit in silence for a moment before he asks, "Can I ask you a question?"

I nod.

"Why New York?"

The question surprises me and I think before I speak. "Why not New York?"

He smiles. "You hated going into Phoenix. Said there were too many people and it smelled terrible. New York City doesn't smell any better."

I shrug, but say nothing. How do I tell him I wanted to get as far away from everyone as I possibly could?

"What about you?" I ask, changing the subject. "Why psychology?"

"I wanted to help people."

It's similar to the answer he gave me when we had breakfast. He's telling the truth, but I can't help the feeling that there is something between the lines he's not telling me.

We stare at each other for a moment before I turn to look around his apartment. I move from the table and wander around his living room as he takes our dirty dishes into the kitchen.

"I'm surprised you have time to cook." I run my fingers over the blanket on the back of his couch.

"I don't have much time these days, but Walt hired another psychologist, so the load should get a little lighter in a couple weeks." He comes out of the kitchen, drying his hands with a towel that he tosses on his shoulder when he's done. "What's that face for?"

I look up from his shoulder to catch his eye. "What face?"

"The face you just made when I mentioned Walt."

I shrug. "There wasn't a face.

"There was a face. You don't like him?"

"I don't know him."

"That doesn't mean you don't have an opinion of him," he says, leaning back, resting on the dining room table.

"I've only met him twice. One of those times, you were there."

"I remember," he says, his brows furrowed. "He's very aggressive. Much more than you'd think a therapist would be, but I promise he's a great person. I wouldn't work for him if he wasn't."

"I know." Charlie would never work for someone he didn't trust.

"Now, he does not hold liquor well," he laughs once. "We usually cap him at one drink. Not that he would do anything...inappropriate. He just gets a little loud."

I don't respond and he watches me until my eyes meet his again.

"I'm sorry if he made you feel uncomfortable."

"You have nothing to apologize for, Charlie," I say.

He looks like he wants to say more, but I see his body physically relax when I say his name, so I take advantage and change the subject.

"Was this your UCLA graduation?" I motion to the picture hanging on the wall above his bookshelf in the corner.

"NYU."

My eyes follow the wall down to the floor. He has a few books on his shelf and some sheet music. His saxophone case is sitting on the floor between his entertainment center and bookshelf.

"Do you still play?" I look back at him.

"Not really, no."

"Why not?"

He doesn't respond.

"How long as it been since you've played?" I ask.

He pauses for a breath before he says, "A little over eight years, I guess."

He hasn't played since I left. I turn away from him, back toward the saxophone that's been neglected. "You should play, Charlie."

He doesn't respond, but I can feel his gaze on my back. I turn my attention back to his apartment, eyeing everything. I stop dead in my tracks when I see something folded neatly on the bookshelf. A lavender tie. One I recognize instantly.

"You were wearing this the day I first saw you," I say quietly, tracing the initials with my finger.

"It was March third."

I turn back to face him. He's still leaning against the table, arms crossed over his chest, watching me carefully.

"What does that have to do with anything?" My voice is so small I don't know how he hears me.

"It was your birthday." He hesitates a moment before he finishes. "I always wear it on your birthday."

I blink back the water in my eyes. "Why?"

"It's the only part of you I had left."

chapter nineteen

then

"Charlie, please? It will be so fun!" I begged as we laid on the grass in my front yard. It was the day before graduation, when we would walk and officially say goodbye to high school.

"Penny, I don't want to go. All the guys have already asked me multiple times if I was going and I said no."

A few weeks ago, Charlie started playing basketball with some seniors at the park. I usually went with him and studied for my finals while they played on Saturday mornings. To be honest, I spent more time studying what was on the court than what was in my textbooks.

One of the guys he played with was having a graduation party. And it just so happened to be Brandon Lee – only the most popular guy in school. He'd had parties before, and we'd heard many wild stories. Like the one of someone streaking down the street that Charlie had reminded me of fifty million more times.

But I had no intention of doing *that* so what was the problem?

I'd never been to a high school party before, and I wanted Charlie to enjoy this with me. Problem was, Charlie hated parties. It wasn't that he was anti-social, he was the most social person I knew. He loved everyone and everyone loved him. Kids were constantly coming up to give him fist pumps or saying hi in the hallway. But, for some reason, he hated parties.

"Please? I've never asked you for anything, Charlie!"

He scoffed and lightly flicked my nose. "You've never asked me for anything? Did I not go to that boy band concert for Sandra's birthday? And I took you to the spring carnival that came in March? And then last week I went – "

"Okay, okay I get it." I rolled my eyes as I rolled onto my side to face him and prop my head on my hand.

"I've asked a lot, I know. But I promise I'll never ask again. Just take me to the party."

He looked at me for a long time before he sighed and stood up. "I'm sorry, Penny, but I'm not going to the party." He looked down at me on the ground with his hands on his hips. "And I don't think you should either. It's not smart. You know there will be drinking. It'll just be a bunch of kids acting stupid."

I stood up to face him and had to tilt my head back to catch his eye. I hadn't realized how much he'd grown in the last year. It hurt my neck to look up at him. I never understood why girls wanted tall guys. Girls were constantly talking about boys in the locker room after gym and height always came up. Six-foot-two seemed to be the number they could all agree on. Once Charlie hit his growth spurt and reached six feet tall, I was even more confused. It was so inconvenient. My neck hurt all the time from looking up at him or kissing him. I was five-seven, so it's not like I was small, but it would be so much easier if we were the same height.

He stood there glaring at me, his eyebrows pinched together and something inside me snapped. I don't know what it was about his argument that made me so angry. Charlie never made me angry. I mean, we'd bicker sometimes, but it was never that serious. We bickered when I wanted to stay in, and he wanted to go out. We'd argue over who got to pick the TV show or the radio station. He might bug me sometimes, but he never made me angry.

But this was making me angry. Because he didn't seem to care that *I* cared.

"We're eighteen, Charlie, this is what you do. You go to parties with your friends. If you don't want to go, I'll just go myself. It's not like we have to do everything together." I turned on my heel toward my front door.

"Penny, come on, we can do something else, just the two of us," he said to the back of my head.

"No. I want to go to the party."

"Why do you want to go so bad?" he asked, running a few steps to step in front of me before I could get inside.

"Because."

"That's a terrible answer."

"Ugh, I just want to, okay?" I turned to face him. "Maybe I just want a night to be a normal teenager."

"What does that mean?"

"It means, we don't have any friends, Charlie."

"We're friends," he said, gesturing between us.

I rolled my eyes. "We don't have any *other* friends. Don't you think it's weird that I don't really know any of the kids we're graduating with because we spend all of our time alone?"

"No, you're my girlfriend. Why wouldn't I want to spend all my time with you?"

Why did he have to be so freaking perfect all the time? It made this ten times harder.

"I just want to go to the party, okay?"

"You still haven't told me why," he said, getting exasperated.

"I just want to hang out with friends."

"Right," he said slowly. "The friends you just told me you don't have."

"Maybe that's the point!" I yelled. He rocked back on his heels surprised by my outburst. I wasn't a loud person. I don't think he'd ever heard me yell until that point. "I feel like I've spent the last four years in a bubble and maybe I just...I feel like I missed out on a normal high school experience. I just want to go have some fun."

"Wow, I'm sorry I was such an inconvenience for the last four years," he said dropping his arms from his hips.

"Charlie," I sighed, getting even more frustrated. I hated miscommunication. "That's not what I meant, and you know it."

"Really, because that's exactly what it sounded like. Like I've been holding you back and you would've had all kinds of amazing high school experiences if it wasn't for me."

"Charlie – "

"Have fun at the party," he said, storming around me to climb up his porch steps. His front door slammed so hard I was afraid it broke.

It was the first real fight we'd ever had. Almost ten years of friendship, two years of dating and we'd never had a fight. It was also the first time he left my house without kissing me on my front porch.

Little did we know, he would never get the chance to kiss me on that porch again.

chapter twenty

I hear the shouting before I even make it into the kitchen for my mid-evening break.

"I told you, I am *fine*, Walker," Dannie yells as I open the kitchen door. She's standing across from Walker, arms crossed, leaning against the counter.

His hands are on his hips, his towel resting on his left shoulder. "I really couldn't care less what you've told me, you don't *look* fine. I'm just trying to help you."

"I don't need your help, I'm fine."

"I swear, Dannie, if you say that word one more time, I'm going –"

"Going to what?" Dannie says, pushing off the counter, getting in his face. "That's your problem, Walker. Always inserting yourself where you don't belong."

"I'm your friend, that's what friends do. You'd know if you'd ever let yourself have any."

She laughs humorlessly. "Right, poor, poor, pitiful Dannie, she's all alone and has no one."

"That's not what I said."

"Guys, just calm down, I'm sure – " I try to help, but they ignore me.

"Just leave me alone, Walker. I'm having a baby, not you. Just butt out!" She turns abruptly and storms out through the back door.

Walker rips the towel off his shoulder and snaps it onto the counter with such force the noise makes me jump.

"Sorry," he says gruffly.

"What was all that about?"

"Dannie being Dannie," he runs an impatient hand down his face. "Is she sleeping okay?"

"What?"

"She just looks so *tired*. She can hardly stand on her feet and when was the last time she played the last set with you? She's been skipping out early for weeks because she doesn't feel good, but she refuses to talk about it. She needs to rest, but she won't listen to me. You know Dannie - if it's not her idea, it's a bad one."

He looks so defeated. Walker is one of the sturdiest people I know, I've never seen him look so disheveled.

"I know she's been tired, but she's pregnant. And she's almost in her third trimester. Isn't that normal?"

He's shaking his head before I'm finished. "My sister wasn't like this when she was pregnant. Tired, sure, but not like this. Dannie can hardly keep her eyes open." He takes a deep breath and glances at the back door. "I'm worried about her."

The timer on the oven interrupts us and Walker sighs. "Don't worry about Dannie," I say, but he looks at me like that is the most ridiculous thing I could ask of him. "I'll go talk to her. We have a few minutes before we're on. Finish your dessert."

He nods once before I follow Dannie into the alley.

She hasn't gone far. She's sitting on the curb, her arms wrapped around her belly.

"Hey," I say as she looks up at me.

"I'm guessing he's in there complaining about me."

"Dannie, come on," I say, taking a seat beside her. "He's just worried about you. Because he cares about you."

"Well, he shouldn't."

"Are you feeling, okay?"

"Not you, too," she groans. "I'm fine."

"It's okay to not be fine, you know."

"Yeah, like you're one to talk," she snaps.

I open my mouth to retort, but she's not wrong. I've never been able to admit when I need help.

"Maybe that's the problem," I say just as much to her as I do myself.

"What?"

"Maybe if I had let people help me, I wouldn't be so…" I gesture to myself, lost for words.

She stares at me for the longest time before she finally sighs. "I'm sorry. I'm fine, I promise."

I know Dannie well enough to know when to keep my mouth shut, so I get to my feet. "Will you tell me if you're not?"

She rolls her eyes. "Penny, I'm having a baby, not dying."

"Walker's right, you've been super tired lately, maybe you should take a few days off."

"Maybe you and Walker should stop talking about me behind my back," she snaps.

"I'm pretty sure Walker said it to your face before he said anything to me. We're your friends, we're worried about you. Just like you worried about me with Charlie."

"Speaking of, how was dinner?"

It's obvious she's trying to change the subject, but I'm not sure pushing her further will do any good so I take the bait. "It was good."

She hooks her arm through mine and pulls me back to the kitchen. "How good?"

"It was really good," I say with a smile.

"Are you going to see him again?" she asks, avoiding Walker's gaze on her as we walk through to the dining room.

I shake my head in his direction, and he sighs before the door swings shut behind us.

I turn my attention back to Dannie and shrug. "I think so? Maybe. I don't know."

"Have you talked to your sister about her wedding?"

"A little. But I haven't decided if I'm going or not. Though, she probably needs an answer soon. It's only three months away."

"Ladies, you're on," Jade comes walking by quickly, barely getting the sentence out before she passes us completely.

"I swear that woman walks in her sleep. I don't think she'd be able to stop moving for two seconds," Dannie complains as she takes her seat at the piano.

We play the last set as flawlessly as always, until the last song when Dannie hits a few wrong notes and plays a little slow. Walker's right, she is tired, but I have no idea how to help her. When the last song ends and the dining room empties, we find ourselves in the kitchen once again.

"Are you okay?" Walker asks, as he rubs Dannie's arm.

She jerks her arm away. "If you ask me that one more time, I'm going to make sure *you're* not okay."

Walker's eyes follow her as she storms out of the kitchen before he pinches the bridge of his nose.

"She'll be okay, Walker. I promise. I'll keep an eye on her."

He nods once. "Come on, I'll walk you two home."

Our walk home is silent. Dannie walks with her arms crossed, clearly annoyed and Walker watches her the whole time like she's about to combust any minute now. When we finally make it to our building, Dannie enters without a word, leaving Walker and me on the street.

"Thanks for walking us home."

"Yeah, no problem," he says quietly. "I'll see you tomorrow. Text me when you're in safe."

I offer him a smile before he walks further down the street to his apartment, hands in his pockets and his shoulders slumped. I climb the stairs to find Dannie standing in front of our door.

"I don't have my key," she says.

I pull my key out but turn to her instead of the door. "What?"

"Someone really wise once told me that sometimes the greatest things in life are the most terrifying."

She scoffs. "What idiot said that?"

"You did."

Her eyes widen for a moment before she relaxes her face. "Well, was I right?"

"I'm still figuring it out," I say honestly.

"Let me know when you do." She grabs the key out of my hand and opens the door, walking straight to her room and shutting the door.

I lock the door quietly and text Walker that we made it inside. He doesn't respond.

Their relationship has been rocky since day one. Jade hired Dannie without telling Walker and I think Walker was annoyed we were paying for another musician. He didn't think I needed an accompanist. Jade disagreed, but she's the primary owner and argued it was ultimately her decision.

Then Dannie came in that first day and Walker was completely smitten. I figured Dannie would jump on it quickly and I'd have to live with the awkward fall-out of a one-night stand, but Dannie surprised me by completely ignoring Walker. At first, I thought she just didn't like him and didn't want to lead him on. Dannie didn't do relationships and Walker is a relationship kind of guy. But as time went on it was harder to determine what was hate and what ...wasn't.

Over the years they melded into this love/hate relationship with each other that somehow works. Then Dannie got pregnant, and everything got messy.

My phone dings with a message, pulling me from my thoughts, and I find Charlie's name glaring at me.

Charlie: Are you busy Monday night? It's your day off, right?

Me: It is. What did you have in mind?

Charlie: I have a few friends in town for a conference. We're all going out.

Charlie: You are included in 'we.'

Charlie: If you want to come.

Me: Was that an invitation?

Charlie: A round-a-bout one, but an invitation, nonetheless.

Me: What time?

Charlie: 8

Me: I can meet you there.

Charlie: I can pick you up...?

It's not a big deal for Charlie to see where I live. There's just something so personal about it. Charlie knows teenage me. He still has this glorified version of me in his head and there's a part of me that wants it to stay that way. I want him to see me as the girl he once knew, the girl we both loved. If he sees where I live, sees who I am now...I don't even want to think about the damage that could cause.

I've caused enough damage in my life.

But maybe Dannie isn't the only one who needs to ask for help.

My thumbs hover over my phone for a solid five minutes before I finally respond.

Me: That would be great.

I send him my address before I change my mind.

Charlie: Great, I'll pick you up at 7:45?

Me: Great.

Charlie: See you Monday! Goodnight, Penny.

Me: Goodnight, Charlie.

chapter twenty-one

then

Charlie text me four times after our fight over the party. I didn't respond to any of them.

I woke up early for graduation day and eventually turned my phone off because I was sick of the notifications.

At the ceremony I easily avoided him as our last names were far apart, but the avoidance couldn't last forever. Much to my dismay, our parents had planned a party for us at Charlie's house. After a million photos and a thousand hugs, my family and I finally went home and walked the short distance to the Wright's house.

Charlie's mom made dinner and we sat around the table like we usually did, only this time I asked Sandra to sit between me and Charlie. I could feel his eyes on me all through dinner, but I refused to look his way.

My avoiding him lasted through dinner, but he found me almost immediately after as Sandra and Kara cleaned off the table and I went out into the backyard, trying to escape our parents' incessant tears and walk down memory lane. Mrs. Wright had already brought out his old baby pictures and my mom quickly ran next door to get mine.

"How long are you going to avoid me?" he asked, grabbing my waist to turn me to face him.

I wish I'd had some clever response, but I didn't. I had kept my distance all day and being this close to him made all my resolve fly right out the window.

"I'm not avoiding you," I said quietly.

"You're a terrible liar," he said, tightening his hold on my waist. "You haven't responded to any of my messages. How long are you going to be mad at me?"

I didn't respond. His eyes were wide and intense, and I couldn't seem to remember why I was mad at him to begin with.

"I'm sorry I got so angry," he said bringing his hand up to brush my cheek. "I just don't think going to the party is smart. We can go do something fun, I promise. I'll even eat your gross powdered donuts with you."

I couldn't help the laugh that escaped.

"Just don't be mad at me anymore," he stepped closer somehow, until there was no distance between us. "I love you," he said, bringing his lips to my ear.

I sighed with defeat. "I'm not mad at you anymore."

He kissed my neck before pulling back to look at me. "Good. So, you won't go to the party?"

"I won't go to the party," I promised.

It was the first time I ever lied to him.

He found me quickly.

Just not quickly enough.

I don't remember much of the party. I remember texting Charlie that Sandra had made plans with me, and I'd see him tomorrow. I told Sandra I was going out with Charlie, and she left to hang out with friends before she had to go back to school. It was all too easy.

The party was insane. I'd never seen so many people in one place. Brandon Lee lived in one of the ritziest neighborhoods in Scottsdale. The house was bright white and had three 2-car garages. The lawn had bright green turf that was so soft I almost thought it was real. There was a small water fountain on the front lawn and garden gnomes lining the path to the front door.

Ostentatious didn't even begin to cover it.

People were playing games I didn't know on the front lawn, but it looked like a human version of hungry hippos catching balloons on skateboards. When I found my way inside, the music was so loud I couldn't hear myself think. I could see people talking more than hear any of them. I walked past couples dancing, kissing, drinking and I'm not sure what else. There was a game of beer pong going on in the kitchen - cheers and excitement I could only see as the music grew louder and louder as I walked through the house.

I continued walking until I found the backyard. The backyard was even more packed than the front. There wasn't just one pool, there were two. The smaller pool sat in the far corner and a small trail of water lead to the larger one that had a diving board, a fake rock waterfall that also had a slide and a volleyball net. There were so many shirtless boys in the pool playing volleyball, my eyes couldn't focus.

"You look lost," a voice said in my ear making me jump. I turned quickly to find a boy a few inches taller than me with brown hair smiling down at me. His eyes were brown. And not a pretty brown. They looked like mud. It's the one thing I've always been able to remember vividly. His voice, his body, his face - it's all a blur, but his eyes...

Dark, dreary, mud brown.

"I just got here," I said.

"Did you come with friends?"

"I drove myself."

He nodded, his smile growing. I'd never seen him before. I don't even think he went to my school. I'd later learn that two other senior classes from two different schools had crashed. I assumed he was from one of those schools.

I honestly don't remember many details after that. I think he told me his name and I shared mine. I know he took me on the dance floor at one point and brought me a drink. The drink is when it gets fuzzy.

I remember stumbling up the stairs and finding myself alone with him in a dark room.

I remember the feel of a body on top of mine and silk sheets beneath me.

I remember tears falling down my cheeks.

I remember not being able to hear my own voice when I said no.

I remember my arms feeling like noodles when I tried to lift them and push.

I don't know how long I laid there before Charlie found me.

I remember his voice so clearly. The music was still loud, the crowds were still screaming, but I could hear him clear as day. Even when he spoke so softly in my ear. "It's okay, I love you, you're okay," over and over again.

He picked me up like I weighed nothing and carried me to his car.

I don't know what happened to my dad's car that I'd parked a few blocks down the street. I think Charlie picked it up the next morning. Or maybe it was towed. I have no idea.

By the time we pulled up to the hospital I was coming back to myself. My brain wasn't as muddled anymore, and I was thinking clearly enough to remember what had happened. I cried, I screamed, I begged him to take me home.

He said no.

He stayed with me the whole time and I remember that I never said thank you.

I was grateful that he made me go. Grateful that he called the police on the party. Grateful there was a report. Even though nothing ever came from it.

I never would've made it out of that night without him.

And I never thanked him for any of it.

chapter twenty-two

now

He's right on time. I'm looking at my phone Monday night when the doorbell rings and it's exactly 7:45. I check myself once more in the mirror before I open the door.

He looks incredible. His dark jeans fit far too well, and his grey t-shirt brightens his eyes. His short curls are particularly messy today and it makes me smile.

"Hey, beautiful, you ready?" he asks.

My cheeks heat at how easily the compliment slips out. I glance down at the outfit I maybe spent ten minutes on. I didn't work hard on it, since I don't have a lot to work with. My fashion sense is simple and always has been. I'm wearing my standard skinny jeans and an oversized, royal blue sweater with my brown hair tied up in a ponytail.

I look up and smile. "I'm ready."

He takes a quick look behind me at the apartment before I shut the door.

"The bar is a little ways, we should probably get a taxi."

"That's fine," I say.

He hails the taxi once we get outside and opens the door for me.

"So," he starts as the taxi driver jerks us onto the road. "How do you usually spend your nights off?"

"Practice. Read. I like to play my violin at Central Park."

He nods. "I was surprised to find you playing. I never would've guessed you'd make a career out of it."

"Me too, honestly. I never thought I was good enough to play professionally."

He shakes his head with a smile. "You were always better than you thought you were."

I'm not sure how to respond, but luckily, he goes on before I have to. "How did you start working at the restaurant?"

"I ran into Jade randomly at a coffee shop. I had my violin with me. She asked what I played then asked me to come audition. I only went because I was broke and couldn't afford another day in the hotel."

"Hotel?" His forehead crinkles.

"Yeah, I got a hotel room for a week when I first moved here. Took all of my graduation money to book it."

"How long did you stay there?"

"Just the week."

"Where did you go after that?" he asks, clearly concerned.

"I stayed at the restaurant for a couple weeks until Dannie came. We got our apartment just a few days after she started."

"Wow. Did anyone know?"

"Walker. He's the chef. And part-owner," I remind him. "He found me the second night. He'd forgotten his wallet and found me laying blankets on the kitchen floor."

"What did he say?"

"Not much. He tried to offer me his spare room, even offered to put down a deposit on an apartment, but I couldn't let him do that." I smile at the memories. "He did come in early to make me dinner and would sometimes leave me breakfast in the fridge."

"Why didn't you take the help?"

"We weren't really close at that point. I was still hesitant around people, especially men," I say looking down at my hands.

"It's not something to be embarrassed about, Penny. It's normal to be distant the first few months."

I look up and smile. "You really do sound like my therapist."

He grins. "I'm glad to know my student loans aren't just for show."

"Loans?" I ask. "Didn't you have a scholarship?" He told me he didn't go that fall, but I still hoped they'd held his scholarship.

"I did, for UCLA. NYU came right out of my pocket. Or the banks pocket."

"Did you like UCLA?" I ask. "As much as you thought you would?"

"Yes and no."

"What do you mean?"

He scrutinizes my face for the longest time before he finally responds. "I wasn't in the best place when I first went to school. I started in January, and I was still moody and angry half the time. It took me a while to let myself have any fun."

"I'm sorry," I whisper.

"There's nothing to be sorry for, Penny. I enjoyed it more near the end. I loved my psychology courses and made a few friends my last year. It wasn't all bad."

He smiles as the driver pulls to a stop. He pays then climbs out of the car to open my door before I can. He doesn't say anything as we walk toward the entrance, but he stops suddenly when we reach the front door.

"It's kind of crowded, I don't want to lose you," he says, a strange look crossing his face.

I'm not sure what he means, so I don't respond. I just wait for him to elaborate.

"Can I...hold your hand?"

He looks uncomfortable and I realize he's afraid of rejection. Afraid I will tell him no - that I don't want him to touch me. I realize that Charlie, the same Charlie that has touched almost every inch of my body at one point, is asking *permission* to touch me.

If I'm honest, there is a part of me that wants to say no. To tell him I'm not ready for this. To tell him I've never held another man's hand and I don't know what this means. To him or to me.

But looking at his face, feeling his breath on my face, I can't form any words. All I can think is that if anyone is allowed to hold my hand it's Charlie.

So, I take a deep breath. And I nod once.

Instant relief fills his features, and he takes my right hand in his so carefully it takes me a second to register the warmth of his hand covering mine and the light squeeze he offers. He stares at our joined hands for one breath, two, before he looks back at me with the most joyful smile on his face. My cheeks warm and I look down at my feet.

I'd be lying if I said my breathing didn't become a little irregular once his fingers wrap around mine. That there isn't a part of my brain making sure I don't hyperventilate. But there is a bigger of me, the part that has thought of Charlie every single day for the last eight years, that finds nothing but comfort in the feel of his touch.

He pulls my hand gently and leads me into the bar.

It seems like everyone is already here. The minute we enter the building all eyes turn towards us. It's a small bar, like Charlie sad it was, it might fit fifty people. And half of those people are yelling Charlie's name.

"Hey man," Charlie says gripping some guy's hand and pulling him into a one-armed bro hug, never releasing his hold on my hand. "Long time."

"Too long," the stranger says. "I'm surprised you even came out tonight. Figured you'd want to avoid-"

Charlie clears his throat and gestures to me. "This is Penny."

The stranger's eyes widen. "Penny."

I smile. "Hi."

He grins suddenly, and offers me his hand. "It's great to meet you, Penny. We have heard, uh, many things about you. I'm Garth."

I take his hand and I can feel Charlie's eyes on my face, waiting for a reaction. "It's nice to meet you."

His hand is warm. It's a firm handshake and his fingers linger around mine a beat too long until Charlie says, "Let me introduce you to everyone."

I'm grateful for the push that makes Garth release my hand with a smile. I might be able to handle Charlie's hand wrapped around mine, but I'm not ready for everyone else's.

The bar is so small, it's impossible not to feel everyone's body heat or get bumped into multiple times. I can't remember anyone's name. It's mostly guys with a few girlfriends thrown in the mix. Everyone he introduces me to seems to know my name already, their eyes lighting up with understanding whenever we're introduced.

"You're not going to forget about me, are you?" A sultry female voice has us turning around.

"Charlotte," Charlie says an odd expression crossing his face.

"Hey, Char," she says, reaching up to wrap her arms around his neck, pulling him so tightly against her, his grip on my hand starts to loosen. I find myself gripping his hand tighter and biting my tongue to refrain from commenting on the ridiculous nickname.

"Where have you been? You never come out anymore," she whines when he pulls away. And I mean, literally whines.

"Just been busy. Work's been a bit hectic."

"Who's this?" she asks, her sharp eyes following his hand.

"Oh, uh," he says, looking more uncomfortable than I've ever seen him. "This is Penny."

Her eyes widen in understanding. "Wow. In the flesh."

She doesn't extend her hand for a handshake or a hug or say it's nice to meet me, but neither do I. We just stand there staring at each other.

Finally, she looks back to Charlie and says, "Do you remember that night in Costa Rica?"

Charlie's eyes grow so wide, I'm sure they're about to pop out of his head. "Yes," he says slowly.

"The guys and I were just reminiscing about the school days and I was telling them about our trip." She turns her attention back to me. "You wouldn't believe the crazy things we did back then. Though it was hard to get Char out of his scholarly shell," she laughs like she's made a joke. "He always took his grades too seriously. Worked harder than everyone else. Rarely ever had any fun."

"That sounds like Charlie," I say as another body bumps into mine and I have to take a deep breath to focus on the conversation in front of me.

"Oh right, you guys went to high school together?"

I nod and Charlie's hand tightens around mine. I don't dare look at him, but I can feel his eyes on me.

"We should talk sometime, share all the juicy Char gossip," she giggles, shooting flirty eyes back at Charlie. "Costa Rica was the wildest I ever got him. I thought I'd have to push him a little, but it didn't take very much coaxing to get him into the water once I undressed."

If I wasn't already tense with social anxiety, I am now. I can feel my chest tighten and I don't want to hear any of this. I take a deep breath trying to calm my racing heart.

It doesn't work.

"We just went skinny dipping, Charlotte," Charlie says. "You don't have to make it sound so scandalous."

"Wasn't it, though?" she says, taking a step closer to him. "I mean, you couldn't keep your hands off me that night."

"Charlotte – " I hear him say, but I pull my hand out of his and head toward the door before I hear the rest of his sentence.

More bodies bump into mine and I'm aware of a few of them apologizing before I burst through the front door and take in a gulp of fresh air. I take a few deep breaths and close my eyes, trying to regulate my breathing.

In...two...three...four, hold.

Out...

"Hey," I hear Charlie come up behind me. "Are you okay?"

I nod, unable to find my voice just yet. He doesn't say anything, and he doesn't try to touch me. He just stands with me waiting for my breathing to regulate.

I shouldn't be shocked. I've been walking the line since I ran into him at the restaurant. Trying to pretend like nothing had changed between us and we could go back to the way things always were. But I'm not the same person I was when I was at eighteen and, clearly, neither is he.

The Charlie I knew would never go skinny dipping, even with me.

Too much has happened, too much has changed. And we can't keep pretending like it hasn't. We can't keep living in this bubble.

"Do you want to leave?" he finally asks when my breathing starts to go back to normal. "We can pick up some food?"

I turn to look at him. "We just got here. Don't you want to see your friends?"

"I'll see them next time."

"Stop," I plead.

"Stop what?"

"Just stop."

He takes a step closer, his hand moving to grab my arm or my hand, but I'm not sure because I take a step back. "Penny – "

"Did you sleep with her?" I know I shouldn't ask, I don't deserve to know the answer. It's an unfair question, but the last eight years have been unfair, what's another question.

"Not exactly." He eyes me carefully before he continues. "We dated my last year at NYU. We messed around, but I promise Penny, we never slept – "

"Stop!" I say firmly before he can finish. "Just stop. You don't owe me an explanation. You don't owe me anything, Charlie. You were a single guy in college, you had every right to sleep with whoever you wanted."

"It's not that simple, Penny."

"Well, it should be," I snap.

He doesn't respond, but he makes no move to go back inside either.

"You're here to see your friends. Go inside and see them. I'll get a taxi."

"You can't take a taxi this late by yourself," he argues.

"I can take care of myself, Charlie."

"I know you can, I wasn't – "

I cut him off again, "No, Charlie, stop. *Please.*" I can feel the tears pooling in my eyes and I try hard to stop them, but they fall anyway.

"Penny, what's wrong?"

I laugh humorlessly. "Me! I'm what's wrong. I'm a mess! I can't even go into a bar and meet your friends without almost having panic attack."

"We don't have to stay."

"Stop it!" I shout. I can see a couple walking into the bar look back at me with wide eyes, but I don't care. "You can't keep doing this."

"Doing what?"

"Trying to fix me!"

He doesn't respond to my outburst. He just stares at me. He doesn't move or try to look away. His eyes never leave mine, but all I can see is eighteen-year-old Charlie looking at me with so much agony in his eyes, like I'm still that damn piece of broken glass.

I have to look away.

"We have been playing house," I say to my feet. "This isn't real. We're not eighteen anymore." I brave a glance and he hasn't moved a muscle. "I'm a mess, Charlie. I'm *broken*. I have this...this ache inside of me that will never go away."

I hold my chest like I might be able to put it back together. I feel the tears fall down my cheeks and onto my fist.

I'm so sick of crying.

"Do you know the last time I went to a bar like this? Never. Because I can't do it. Because I still hate people touching me. Walker hasn't even touched me! He won't even give me a hug, because he knows how much I hate it and he's one of my best friends."

The tears are falling so fast my vision is becoming blurry.

"You deserve better. You shouldn't have to leave your friends because I'm uncomfortable or feel the need to explain any of your past relationships. You shouldn't be surprised when I say yes when you ask me out." I wipe away the tears, but more follow too quickly and I can't wipe them away fast enough. "You shouldn't have to ask me if you can hold my hand," I whisper the last words, my voice gone now.

"Penny, I – "

"Please," I say, closing my eyes tightly for two breaths. "Stay with your friends. I'll get a taxi home."

I open my eyes again and he stares at me for the longest time, pain etched in every one of his features. I know he wants to argue with me, but I'm not sure he knows what to say.

"I'll call Walker," I say, hoping that will pacify him. "He'll pick me up."

He nods once, relief clear in his eyes, but he still doesn't say anything.

"Goodnight, Charlie," I say, turning away. I'll wait on the curb.

"I'm not trying to fix you, Penny," he says before I can even take a step. I turn back to face him, and he still hasn't moved. His hands are hanging loosely at his sides and there is so much emotion on his face I couldn't pinpoint one feeling if I tried. "I'm not trying to fix you," he says again. "I'm just..." his eyes scan my face, my body, back up again before he finally speaks. "You're not broken, Penny. And I don't want to fix you. I just want you back."

He doesn't give me a chance to respond before he walks back toward the bar.

There's a part of me that wants to follow him. To ask all the questions racing through my mind. But I can't go back in there. So, I sit on the corner curb and call Walker like I promised.

It doesn't take him long to get here and my tears have dried by the time he pulls up. I'm not sure where he was, but he's here within fifteen minutes. He opens the taxi door for me and before I climb in, I take one last look at the bar to find Charlie sitting on the bench outside watching me. When I climb in the taxi and drive off, I see him walk back inside. Like he was waiting to make sure Walker came. To make sure I was okay.

"Thanks for coming," I say, looking out my window at the city lights as we drive through the busy night.

"Of course," he says. "Are you okay?"

I nod.

"You can talk about it if you want to."

I turn to face him and he's already looking at me. I'm not sure what it is, how I know, but I can tell by the look in his eyes that he knows everything.

Dannie must've told him. I should probably be angry she's airing my dirty laundry, but instead I'm just grateful there's one less person I have to put on a façade for.

"Am I ever going to be normal?" I finally ask.

"What do you mean?"

"It's been almost nine years," I laugh humorlessly. "I shouldn't cringe every time a man wants to shake my hand or pat my arm. I should be able to go into a bar without having a panic attack."

"I don't think you ever just...get over it, Penny."

"I've been in therapy for eight years. *Years.* I go to a support group two or three times a week and I don't feel like anything's changed." I look down at my hands.

"I wouldn't say nothing's changed, you're not the same person I met eight years ago."

"What do you mean?" I ask, looking at him again.

"Penny, when I first met you, I thought Jade was crazy for hiring you. You didn't speak, you wouldn't look me in the eye. You avoided the kitchen and used to eat dinner outside on the curb. You wouldn't talk to anyone when Jade tried to introduce you. You were..." he can't seem to find the right word, but I can.

"Broken."

He looks at me with sad eyes, but he doesn't correct me.

"I don't know when you started therapy or going to the support group, but I think it helped. One day, a few weeks after you started, you came in and said good morning to me. I dropped my chicken parm. I was so shocked you actually said something to me," he laughs.

"I remember that. Marinara sauce flew everywhere. It was covering your pants," I smile.

"Yeah, I never got the stain out. I had to throw them out."

We laugh together at the memory before he continues.

"You started talking a lot more. When Dannie was hired, you started coming back into the kitchen to eat your dinner. You'd ask about mine and Dannie's days and you'd talk about yours. It was like you'd finally found yourself."

I tried to look at the last eight years from his perspective. I don't think I realized how big of a mess I was when I came here. I just wanted to get out of Scottsdale. Get away from Charlie. He needed to live his life and I needed to find mine. But I was still hurting – trying to cope with what had happened. And I wasn't doing a very good job.

The taxi pulls in front of my building and Walker pays the fee.

"You don't have to pay, I asked you to come all the way across town to get me."

"I was close, it's no big deal."

"Where were you anyway?" I ask as we stop in front of my building.

He sighs. "I was at labor and delivery with Dannie."

"What? Is she okay?" Panic swells inside me.

"She's fine. So is the baby. It was Braxton hicks, but she wasn't sure."

The panic immediately deflates and turns into confusion. "And she went to the doctor?"

He laughs once. "Not willingly, but I finally got her there. She's mad at me, of course, because it was nothing."

"Yeah, but you didn't know it was nothing."

He just shrugs his shoulder. "She's inside. She insisted on getting her own cab home so I could come get you." He turns to leave. "Text me when you're inside."

"Walker?"

He turns his head toward me with eyebrows raised.

"Will you give me a hug?" I ask quietly.

I'm not sure when I decided or what made me finally ask. I've thought about it over the years, but never plucked up the courage to actually ask. If there's anyone I can trust it would be Walker, but in all the time I've known him he's never once touched me.

He touches other people all the time. He puts his arm around Jade sometimes when they walk through the crowd at the restaurant, or he'll give her a hug at the end of the night. He'll put a hand on Dannie's lower back when we walk down the street or rub her arms when she's stressed, but he's never touched me.

His eyebrows go higher and there is a moment of surprise and hesitation before his face relaxes and he smiles. He takes a small step forward and wraps his arms lightly around me as I weave mine around his waist, my cheek falling on his shoulder.

I close my eyes tightly and take two deep breaths, counting to four, before I realize I don't need to. That I'm not afraid or uncomfortable. That it actually feels nice.

Comforting.

Friendly.

Loving.

I squeeze him once before I lean back. "Thanks, Walker."

"Anytime." He glances up toward our window, toward Dannie, before he smiles at me once more. "Let me know how she is."

"She may act like she's made of stone, but she's not," I say. "Just give her time."

He looks up once more at the window, exhaling. "I'd give her the world, Penny."

He squeezes my hand before turning and walking away.

I can still feel his hand in mine when I walk up the stairs and when I crawl under the covers and shut off the lights, I think back to our hug and the memory, the feeling, of being held washes over me and I realize I might want to do that again.

chapter twenty-three

then

The days that followed were the worst days of my life. I think they were even worse than the party itself. At least half the party was fuzzy, and I didn't remember many details.

Nothing about the aftermath was fuzzy.

My parents were fighting all the time, mostly about me. My dad wanted to send me to therapy, my mom said she wouldn't force me. My dad would try to pull me out of my room and my mom would say to leave me alone.

Sandra was gone most of the time. Whether she was spending time with friends or just trying to hide from the fighting, I don't know. I never asked where she went. I didn't say much the first couple weeks. I'd nod my head when my mom asked if I was hungry or shake my head when I was sick of her questions.

I spent most of my time in my room, coming out only to use the bathroom or to find a glass of water. No one bothered me much. I don't think anyone knew what to say to me.

Except Charlie.

Charlie spent almost every day with me that summer. Mostly in my room. The first couple days he didn't say much. He just sat on the floor, leaning against my bed, where I curled into a ball and cried. On day three he told me we had to tell my parents. When he'd brought me home from the hospital, I think he told them I got a stomach bug or something, I'm not sure. After two days he told me we had to tell them the truth.

So, we did. Or Charlie did.

We gathered in the living room, and I sat on the couch, holding my knees close to my chest. Everyone's eyes were on me, waiting for me to say the words I'd never get out again. I think at one point I looked at Charlie for help because he finally said what I couldn't.

My mom cried, my dad yelled. Sandra sat in shock for a few moments before she finally asked if she could hug me, and I nodded. We sat in the living room for hours before I quietly excused myself back to my room.

My parents fighting started shortly after and I hid in my room with Charlie for weeks.

He came over almost every day after breakfast and would often stay until dinner. Some days he would read a book out loud, other days he would bring his saxophone and try to get me to play my violin with him. I never did and he never played either. Mostly though, he just sat with me. He'd stop reading or talking when he noticed tears were running down my cheeks.

I knew he wanted to hold me, but he never tried. Whenever I started crying, he'd just sit down on the floor and lean his head against my mattress. He wouldn't say a word. He'd just let me cry.

Time moved slow and fast all at once. Before we realized it was mid-August. Sandra was getting ready to go back to school and as far as I knew Charlie was, too.

Until I overheard him talking to my parents.

"I can push it off a year, it's not a big deal. I was already considering it...before," Charlie said. "I want to work and save some money."

"You have a full ride scholarship. What do you need to save money for?" I heard my dad ask. "If you defer a year, will they hold your scholarship?"

Only silence followed.

"Honey, I know you mean well, but you can't give up your scholarship," my mom said.

"I can't leave her," he argued, and I could feel my heart breaking in my chest.

"Have you talked to your parents about this?" my dad asked.

"Not yet, but it's not their decision to make, it's mine. I'm not leaving her."

"Charlie, I really think you should talk to your parents about this," my mom said. "Don't make any rash decision."

"She's not getting better," he croaked. I don't think I'd ever heard him sound so sad before. Defeated.

"She will," my mom said. I could almost see her rubbing his arms, soothingly. "It just takes time."

"I don't know how to help her." I could hear the tears in his voice.

That was when I stopped listening. I closed my bedroom door and curled myself into a ball on my bed. I didn't want to hear anymore.

Charlie was going to stay in Scottsdale. He was putting off school. He was putting off UCLA. The school he'd been dreaming about his entire life. He was giving up a full ride scholarship.

For me.

I felt sick.

A few minutes later there was a soft knock on my door.

"Come in," I said.

"Hey," he said with a smile as he came in, shutting the door behind him. If I hadn't heard him, I wouldn't have even noticed how puffy his face was under his eyes or how bloodshot they were. It was obvious he'd been crying, probably for days. He had facial hair I hadn't noticed until then, like he hadn't shaved in a while. And his curls were flying every which way like his hands had run through them a million times. It looked messy.

Charlie never looked messy.

"Your parents are going out."

Going out. Like I didn't know they were meeting with a marriage counselor. They started going not long after they found out and started fighting about me. I don't know what they expected to come of it since the fighting only got worse, but they went every week. They hadn't told me they were seeing a counselor, but I'd overheard them talking about it a couple weeks after graduation.

"I thought maybe we could go for a walk. It's nice out," he said. Only in Arizona would a 95-degree day in August be considered "nice."

I wanted to say no. I wanted to stay in bed and tell him to leave. But then I remembered what I'd just heard.

She's not getting better.

I'm not leaving her.

I eventually nodded and let him get me my shoes out of my closet and the house keys off my nightstand.

"It hasn't been all that hot this year. Next year will probably be terrible," he said as he climbed down the front porch steps.

But I couldn't do it.

"You have to go to school, Charlie," I said, stopping on the porch.

He looked up at me with surprise in his eyes. "What?"

"I heard you talking to my parents. You have to go to school."

He sighed and turned his body fully toward mine. "I'm just putting it off a year, it's not a big deal."

"You're not just putting it off, you're giving up a full ride scholarship. You need to go to school."

"Penny, we can talk about this later. Please? Let's just go for a walk, okay?"

"No," I insisted. "You have to go to school."

I turned and walked back into the house and wasn't surprised to find that he'd followed me.

"Penny, I'm just trying to help you."

I stopped in my tracks and turned to face him.

"I don't need your help," I protested.

He opened and closed his mouth a few times like he was trying to find the right words, but never did.

"Go home."

"Penny, please – "

"I don't need you, Charlie," I said it as firmly as I could even though it couldn't have been further from the truth.

I could tell my words hurt, though he tried to hide it.

"It's okay to need someone. I just want to be here for you."

"Now you want to be here for me? Where were you eight weeks ago?"

He looked like I'd kicked him. He just stood there, watching me, the pain clear on his face.

"It was supposed to be you," I whimpered as tears started blurring my vision. I knew what I was saying was mean. Wicked. But it was the only way I knew to handle it. To make him leave. To realize I was a broken mess and he deserved better.

"I know," he whispered and that was the breaking point. It felt like a bullet to my chest. I never knew you could physically feel your heart break until then.

Charlie was never quiet. Ever. He was bold, powerful, strong. Everything but quiet.

"I'm so sorry, Penny," his croaked.

"Stop," I closed my eyes tightly, shaking my head.

"Stop what?"

"Stop apologizing!" My voice was rising, and I looked up to see a surprised look on his face. Not even surprised; scared. Afraid. "I am so sick of everyone apologizing!" I yelled even louder.

It was the first moment after the party that I actually felt angry. For the most part I had just felt sad, lost, confused, and extremely depressed. I'd never gotten angry. But as my breathing became erratic and my hands started to shake, all I could feel in that moment, throughout my entire body, was anger.

I was angry at Charlie for apologizing when he was the only person that had made anything better. Angry at him for not touching me. Angry at myself for not letting him. Angry that he was still trying so hard to help me when I'd given him every reason to walk away. Angry that he was willing to give up everything for me. Angry at him for looking at me with so much sadness and pity in his eyes, I wanted to throw something at him.

Just *angry*.

"Penny – "

"No! You promised me, Charlie!" I yelled so loud my own ears rang.

I didn't have to say what I meant. He knew and I could see the change happen in his eyes right there. The guilt he'd carried since that night. Guilt that somehow what happened to me was his fault.

And I'd just validated that guilt with four little words.

"You promised!" I yelled again, grabbing a random knickknack off the entry table. I threw it at him before I could process what I was doing.

He didn't even try to doge it. It hit him square in the chest. Blood starting soaking into his shirt, but he didn't move a muscle. He didn't flinch. He didn't duck or try to move away. He just stood there and took it. Like he wanted the punishment.

"You said that you would make love to me!"
Another throw.
"You promised that you would be my first!"
Another.
"You broke your promise, Charlie!"

I was all out of things to throw, and I couldn't seem to stand anymore, my legs unable to carry the weight, and I fell to my knees. Tears soaked the front of my shirt, snot ran down my face. I'm sure I looked terrible. Broken.

I felt broken.

I could feel him as he knelt next to me. He didn't try to touch me, but I could still feel him. I think I knew, even then, that no matter where we were, whether we were together or hundreds of miles apart, I would always feel him.

"I'm so sorry," his voice cracked. I looked up just enough to see tears fall at his knees.

We sat there for what felt like hours. Just crying together.

That night, after he left, I packed a bag and booked a bus ticket. I left the next morning and didn't look back.

chapter twenty-four

now

He doesn't try to contact me for over a week after the fiasco outside the bar. Work has picked up and the dining room is loud and busy. Walker has been in a frenzy for days trying to keep up, constantly complaining that we need to hire kitchen hands. Dannie reminds him that he's too hard to work with and no one would last.

Jade's been in the worst mood, but no one can figure out why. We've been booked in advance every night the last two weeks, but she's been on a rampage. I've spent the majority of my time keeping her and Dannie away from each other. They already hate each other when they're in good moods. I can't imagine what would happen if they were both cranky.

On Friday night, Jade comes in with a smile.

"I just booked the last table. We are officially booked tonight."

"That's great," Walker says. "Who is it?"

"Dr. Jones. I called him myself and extended a personal invitation this morning. Said we would give the whole table free dessert."

Walker and Dannie both look at me.

I clear my throat and turn to Jade. "Do you know who he's bringing?"

"He said he would treat his whole staff to dinner. Isn't that wonderful?" She claps her hands together in front of her before hustling off to her office.

"Is he coming tonight?" Dannie asks once she's gone.

"I don't know."

"Are you okay?" Walker asks.

I nod. "I'm fine. I promise."

"I can play alone if you want to go home," Dannie offers.

"No. This is my job. I'm not going to run away just because he might show up," I say.

Dannie looks like she wants to argue with me, but Walker gives me an encouraging smile and squeezes my arm before Jade barges in announcing that it's five o'clock.

I take a deep breath as I enter the dining room and quickly scan the crowd. About half the tables have arrived, which is normal. The tables don't usually fill until around seven. Some people like to eat dinner extremely late.

Dannie and I play the first set and it's anything but perfect. She comes in late in the second movement, and I hit too many wrong notes, my eyes scanning the dining room, looking for a head of curls instead of my sheet music.

It's not until we're halfway through our third set that I see him. He's wearing a navy-blue suit, he must've come straight from the office.

His finds me quickly. His eyes searching the room for just a moment before landing on me.

I'm not sure what I play in the thirty seconds that we stare at each other, but he's the one to eventually break eye contact and join his colleagues. I watch him as he says hello to Dr. Jones and the rest of the table I don't know. He removes his suit jacket, placing it on the back of his chair before he sits down and begins to roll his sleeves to his elbows.

I play on autopilot as I'm taken back to a random memory from senior year. It was a Saturday morning and he'd just finished his basketball game. He sat next to me on the park bench, smelling way too good for a teenage boy drenched in sweat. I'd made a silly comment about how good his forearms looked and he laughed. I guess a girl had never told him how sexy forearms were. I don't think I had realized myself until that moment. After that, he would randomly flex his arms or dramatically drape his arms around me, making fun of me.

The memory has me smiling and all the stress in my body evaporates. Once our piece is done, before I can even comprehend what I'm doing, I walk up to his table.

"Dr. Jones, it's great to see you again." I turn my attention toward the doctor, feeling the heat of another gaze on my face.

"Always a pleasure. Charles here has been telling me all week we should come back. He even paid for the entire table," Dr. Jones says, gesturing toward Charlie.

I turn to the man sitting to my right.

"You paid for the whole table?"

He doesn't say anything.

"You were a little chaotic up there tonight. Are you feeling all right?" Dr. Jones pipes up.

"She played fine," Charlie snaps.

"It was just a bit rocky," Dr. Jones says.

Charlie opens his mouth to retort, but Dannie interrupts us.

"Dr. Jones, is it?" she says, taking the seat next to him making his eyes go wide. "I've heard a lot about you. You've come to see Penny so many times, I'm starting to get offended you haven't asked about me." She tosses her hair flirtatiously over her shoulder catching my eye. I give her a look of gratitude before I turn to Charlie.

"Can we talk?" I ask while Dannie has Dr. Jones distracted.

His shoulders sag with relief and his entire body seems to relax as he stands. "Please."

"Is it too late to meet when I get off?"

He shakes his head. "Not at all. What time?"

"I should be home by midnight. My place?"

"I'll be there."

I take the stairs slowly. I pull my phone out of my pocket to check the time, 12:10.

"Hey," I hear as I take the last step to my floor. I look up from my phone to see Charlie sitting on the floor, leaning against my door.

"You said midnight, right?" he says, when I don't say anything.

"Yes, right. Sorry I'm late."

"It's okay," he says, standing. He looks disheveled. His tie is loosened, and the top two buttons of his shirt are undone. His jacket is draped over his arm, his shirt is untucked, and his sleeves are rolled up to his elbows. It's not a look I've seen on him much, and the sight has a lump forming in my throat.

We don't speak as I open the door and take off my shoes. He takes his off as well and places them next to mine. He looks around the room, taking everything in. Not that there's much to take in. Dannie and I never got around to decorating. There's nothing on the walls except a poster Dannie got at some music festival a few years back.

"You've lived here the whole time?" he asks, and I nod.

"Just one room?" He nods toward the bedroom door.

"Yeah, it's Dannie's."

"Where do you sleep?"

"The couch."

"You sleep on the couch?" he asks as his eyebrows come together. "Every night?"

"It's a pull-out, it's not bad."

He nods, but it's clear he doesn't believe me. "Is she here?"

"No," I say. "She's staying at Walker's."

It was her idea to give us the apartment. She didn't even ask Walker. She just grabbed his arm and pulled him out of the kitchen before he could ask any questions.

"Look, I uh..." I start, but I have no idea how to have this conversation.

"I'm sorry about the other night," he says and suddenly I'm angry again.

"I swear if you apologize one more time," I shake my head. "There is nothing for you to be sorry for Charlie, there never was."

"What do you want from me, Penny?"

"Honestly? I have no idea," I say, sitting on the couch.

He doesn't wait for an invitation before he sits next to me. There is enough distance he isn't touching me, but if I wanted, I could easily press my leg to his.

"I know you don't want me to apologize, but I do feel like I should apologize for Charlotte. She shouldn't have said what she said. She was just trying to get under my skin. She didn't take the break-up well."

"Can I ask you something?" I ask, tentatively.

"Of course."

"When I asked you if you'd slept with her, you said not exactly. What does that mean?"

He sighs and looks down at his hands.

"We started dating the end of my first year at NYU. We'd been in the same social circle for a while. I knew she was interested, but I hadn't really dated anyone." He fidgets with the bottom of his shirt. "Garth had planned a welcome barbeque that first week and kind of set us up. We started dating. If you could even call it that. We rarely saw each other, school was hectic, and I was never really that into her. I know that makes me terrible, but I didn't know how to handle it."

"It doesn't make you terrible," I say, and he smiles at me before continuing.

"Anyway, she started getting more handsy and I knew she wanted to take it to the next level, but... I just couldn't do it."

"Why not?" I ask quietly.

"I couldn't stop thinking about you."

"Me?" I say with real surprise in my tone. His last year at NYU was nearly five years after I left.

He nods. "I made you a promise, Penny, and it wasn't just because I wanted to give you whatever you wanted. It's because I wanted you to be *my* first."

It takes a minute for his words to sink in.

I don't think I ever realized how Charlie was affected in all of this. Not really. I was the one who was assaulted, not him, but his life changed, too. Almost as much as mine did. He had a life planned, a life with me. And it was taken away.

I took it away when I left.

The thought brings tears to my eyes. This is exactly what I didn't want. I left because I thought that would make his life easier. He would go to UCLA like he planned and buy the suburban home in Arizona when he graduated. He'd be happy.

"I'm so sorry, Charlie," I whisper.

"Now who's apologizing when they shouldn't?" He looks at me with eyebrows raised and a small smile on his lips. "Anyway, we never went all the way. It was the night in Costa Rica when I finally broke up with her. She'd convinced me to go skinny dipping. I was frustrated and lonely and I thought, 'why not?' I was also extremely naïve and inexperienced. I thought she just wanted to swim," he laughs once.

"Anyway, I eventually told her I didn't want to. She got mad, we didn't really see much of each other after that, but we ran in the same circles, so it was inevitable."

He doesn't look away, waiting for my response.

I take a deep breath and give him the answers he deserved all those years ago.

"I always thought it would never leave me, you know," I start, and his eyes focus on my face even more, eyebrows turned up in a moment of surprise that I'm actually talking about it.

"I always thought that no matter where I went or what I did, I would...see him, *feel* him in everything, everywhere."

I can feel his breathing become erratic. Even after all this time, it still makes him angry. I look over at his hand rested on his thigh to see it in a tight fist and his knuckles are turning white.

"It didn't though," I continue, staring down at my hands. "I started therapy when I moved to the city and joined a support group shortly after. It really helped. I have therapy every Tuesday and Thursday and a support group every Saturday. I was really nervous to go in the beginning, but it's... I think it's ultimately what helped me move on. As much as I could anyway."

"You told me there was an ache inside of you, you thought would never go away."

I look up at him. "I wasn't talking about him."

His inhale is sharp, and he looks at me in disbelief, though I'm not sure why. He knows how I felt about him.

"I didn't carry him with me, Charlie, I carried *you.* It was you I saw everywhere I went. Every time I saw someone with blonde hair or glasses, I thought it was you. In the beginning I hoped it was you. I think there was a part of me that always wanted you to find me."

"I should've been there, I should've – "

I'm already shaking my head. "It's not your fault, Charlie."

"I broke my promise to you, Penny," his voice breaks and I realize for the first time that maybe he's still a little broken, too.

I wasn't the only one who left Arizona in pieces.

"I never should've said those things before I left."

His hand goes to his chest rubbing a spot I can't see, but I wonder if he has a scar from the things I threw at him that night.

"That day...of the party." He glances at me through his eyelashes, waiting for my reaction before he continues.

I nod once, encouraging him.

"Why did you want to go so bad? I never understood why you were so adamant to go."

I'd thought about this so much over the years. It was just a party, a high school party even. It was stupid how badly I wanted to go, but at eighteen it made sense.

I take a deep breath and look at the floor.

"I don't know. I guess I was just...scared. Graduation seemed to sneak up on us and you were going to school in California. It seemed so far away at the time." I laugh once at the thought. It wasn't nearly as far as New York. "Everything was changing and I just, I got nervous that I'd put all my eggs in your basket and if you left..." I take another breath. "I guess the party was this warped way of me making myself feel like I had a life outside of you. Like if you left I had enough in my life that I could live without you." I lean my head back on the couch and turn to look at him.

"Why didn't you ever come back? Or call?" he whispers. I hate when he whispers; when he's quiet. It's such an unnatural reaction for him, I can tell how much all of this hurts him. How much *I* hurt him.

"Charlie..." I stand with a sigh, moving to stand by the window.

"It's been over eight years, Penny." He speaks loudly, now, firm. "I've spent almost a decade trying to figure out what I could've done differently. Thinking that if I hadn't pushed you so hard, maybe you wouldn't have walked away or if I had just given you more space." He stands forcefully, running his hands down his face.

"Charlie..." I say again.

He turns toward me. "I understand why you left; I never blamed you for that, but why couldn't you have called? Why couldn't you tell me you were leaving? Why couldn't you just say goodbye?"

"Because everything was broken!" I yell at him. "Everything around me fell apart. My parents were on the verge of divorce, Sandra couldn't even be in the house anymore, around me. Everything was broken because of me! I wasn't going to break you, too."

"And you think leaving didn't break me?" he yells back. "Penny, I wouldn't have judged you for wanting to get out of that town. I would've helped you; I would've gone with you."

"That's the problem! Your whole life was ahead of you. You had a scholarship for crying out loud! And you were going to drop it to stay in Scottsdale with me. I couldn't do that to you," I take a few deep breaths, trying to calm myself. "And look at you." I say quietly. "You did it. You bought a condo, you got your master's degree. You did all of it, Charlie. Without me."

He scoffs. "Without you? Penny, everything, I did was because of you."

He takes two steps forward.

"Do you know why I became a psychologist? Because I never knew how to help you and I hated that feeling. I hated feeling so completely...powerless. *Helpless.* I wanted to help people like you. I took the job with Walt because his network is strictly victims of sexual assault."

It takes me a minute to register what he's said. He had always talked about UCLA for their band program. I just assumed that's what he studied. Even after he told me he hadn't played his saxophone in years, I couldn't think of him doing anything else. Nothing else made sense. When he told me he was a psychologist, I figured he'd double majored or something. I left so he wouldn't give it up. But he did. Because he wanted to help me.

Because he wanted to help everyone.

He takes a few more steps, closing the distance between us and I feel a tear fall down my cheek and watch it land on his hand that's reaching toward me. He doesn't seem to notice.

"Everything I did was because of you. For you. I wanted to give you everything."

"Why?" I whisper.

He takes another step closer until there's no more space between us and carefully brings his hand to my cheek. He's moving slowly, watching my eyes for any indication that I want him to stop. When I don't move, he does. I feel the heat from his fingers first before they finally brush a tear from my cheek and it's the most incredible feeling in the world. I surprise both of us when I lean into his touch instead of away from it. His hand moves to cup my whole cheek.

"Because you deserved a good life, Penny. And I wanted to be the one who gave it to you."

"You deserved better than me. You still deserve better," I say, closing my eyes tightly. Hiding the only way I know how.

He reaches up to put his other hand on my cheek and his thumbs carefully brush over my closed lids until I open them.

"There isn't better than you," he whispers and pulls me into his body, wrapping his arms tightly around me.

It takes me a second to move, but the beat of his heart under my ear and his hands rubbing my back is everything I didn't know I needed, and suddenly I'm wrapping my arms around his waist.

I don't know how long we stand there, holding each other, but eventually he kisses my forehead and tells me he'll call me in the morning.

"No," I say, grabbing his wrist. "Stay."

His eyes widen, surprised by my request.

"Not like that," I say, feeling the blush crawl up my neck. "I just want you here."

I can't let him go now. Not after we've truly found each other again.

He nods once. "Okay."

We stand there looking at each other for a moment, not sure how this goes.

Finally, I pull him toward the couch, and he helps me pull it out. I drape a couple blankets over the top and climb in. I don't change into pajamas, I don't brush my teeth, I just climb under the covers in my jeans and sweater.

He takes off his tie and unbuttons the top button of his shirt before sliding in next to me and turning on his side to face me.

"Can I ask you something?" I say after minutes of silence.

He nods.

I take a deep breath and brave the question. "Why didn't you ever sleep with me?"

His eyes widen in surprise a little before he controls his face. I'm sure it's the last thing he expected me to ask.

"At the lake house, senior year. Why didn't you do anything? I was more than willing."

He sighs heavily, closing his eyes. "Penny..."

"I'm sorry," I say, moving to lay on my back. "You don't have to answer that. I don't really have a right to be asking you anyway, I'm the one who left."

"You can ask me anything."

I turn my head to see he's still looking at me.

"I loved you so much," he says, moving his hand to my temple, tracing circles. "I wanted you so bad. There were days I couldn't think of anything else. All I could think about was being with you."

He pauses, eyes moving over my face, searching for something.

"I never understood why you were with me. I was high-strung and overbearing. I was impatient. Neurotic. I kept waiting for the day you realized what life had to offer outside of me and you'd leave. I was terrified to go to UCLA without you, afraid you'd find someone while I was away. That's why I started considering other options. I knew it would be the worst thing that would ever happen to me if you left, but I figured if I slept with you, it would be that much harder."

His fingers are still making circles on my temple, and I move my hand to wrap around his.

"I never wanted to leave you," I say quietly.

"I know," he says, but it doesn't reach his eyes. I never knew how scared he was of my leaving. The one thing he always feared the most I made happen.

"Do you?" I ask.

He doesn't answer and I can feel the tears pooling in my eyes again. He wipes a tear that falls down my cheek before it can hit my pillow.

"I do now," he says, finally. "But for a long time, I thought you left because of me."

"I did," I say, "but not for the reasons you think."

"I know," he says again and this time I think he means it.

I close my eyes as his finger starts making circles on my temple again. I'm almost asleep when I feel his lips press against my forehead and he whispers something that sounds a lot like, "I love you."

chapter twenty-five

now

I wake up slowly. It's bright in the apartment so it must be late morning. I turn over groggily and collide with a body.

"Sorry, did I wake you?" Charlie says, his hand grazing my cheek.

"It's okay." I catch his eyes and he smiles at me. His hair is messy from sleep, and he hasn't put his glasses on yet. "Why are you awake?"

"Your phone kept beeping, I'm surprised you didn't hear it," he says. "I turned the ringer off, I hope that's okay."

"It's fine, it's probably Dannie. I told her I would text her when you left. She's at Walker's place."

"I think it's Sandra, actually," he says, holding my phone out to me.

It is Sandra. It's also 10am. We slept for 9 hours.

I open my phone to find six unread messages. Four from Sandra, two from my mom.

"Ugh," I groan and toss the phone aside.

"Is everything okay?" he asks, moving his hand up to rest behind his head.

"They want to know if I'm coming to the wedding. They need a head count."

"Are you going to go?" he asks.

"I don't know," I sigh, throwing my hands over my eyes.

"I'll go with you. If you want."

I look at him through my fingers. "Weren't you going to go anyway?"

"Honestly, no. I mean, I love Sandra, I just didn't know if I could get away from work. But I'll go if you want me there."

"What about work?"

"I'll figure it out."

"You'd do that for me?"

"I'd do anything for you."

I remove my hands completely from my face to look at him and suddenly notice he took his shirt off at some point in the night. The blankets bunch at his waist where the top of his underwear peaks out.

Charlie was never pure muscle, but he wasn't soft either. He worked out, that much you could tell. He didn't have a six pack or anything, but he was the most beautiful boy I'd ever seen.

It's obvious he still works out. I carefully lift my finger to his belly button, and he shivers slightly at the touch, but he doesn't tell me to stop so I keep going. There may not be a six pack, but his muscles are tight, faintly defined. I trace over his stomach lightly with my finger moving up to his chest where there is a small, indented scar that makes an almost perfect circle. I trace it carefully.

"Is this...?" I ask and he nods. I was right, he did have a scar from the things I'd thrown at him. "I'm sorry."

"It's okay," he says as I move my finger up over his collarbone, up his neck and down his jaw until my finger rests lightly on his lips.

I don't move. My fingers hover over his mouth and my breathing becomes frantic. But not in the way it usually does. There is no panic attack forming.

I just want to be closer to him.

"Take whatever you want, Penny," he says quietly.

"What do you mean?" I ask, my heart beating so hard the neighbors could probably hear it.

"Show me what you want."

He holds his hand out for me to take. I stare at it for a few seconds before I carefully wrap my fingers around his.

"You can put my hands where you want them. Wherever you're comfortable with me touching you. You're in control."

I look up and find his eyes on mine and suddenly I want to give him everything.

He knows better than anyone why I don't like being touched. The lack of control, the vulnerability, the submission. And without me having to explain, he understands and he's giving me an out to all of that.

He's putting me in charge.

I pull his hand up and place it on my cheek and I can feel him sigh more than hear it. Like a quick release of air he was holding in. It encourages me to move a little closer until our chests brush and I can feel his heart rate accelerating.

"What else do you want?" His voice is deep, husky. I lift up and rest my forearm on his chest so I can see him better, his hand never leaving my face. I reach down and take his other hand that's resting on his stomach and place it on my hip. We lay there for a moment, and I realize that I have a man's hands on me and I'm not afraid. Not only am I not afraid; I want more.

"Charlie?"

"Yes?"

"Kiss me."

He doesn't have to be told twice. His lips touch mine softly. He's gentle and slow. He's pacing himself, not wanting to scare me – giving me the opportunity to push him away. But he's not scaring me and I want more.

I need more.

I pull his face closer to mine and he reacts quickly. His hands squeeze my waist and pull me over until I'm completely on top of him, my legs straddling his hips. His tongue brushes mine and I forgot how good he tastes. My hands tighten in his hair.

He breaks his lips away and moves down until his breath is tickling my collarbone.

"Is this okay?" he asks.

I nod, unable to find my voice. I feel his tongue brush my neck and I can't seem to get close enough to him. My arms hurt from hanging on so tight and when his lips find mine again, I think I might pass out from the overload of sensations.

He breaks away suddenly, breathing heavily. "We don't have to, Penny, we can go slow – "

I cut him off with a kiss. "No. Don't stop." I kiss his jaw. "Please."

He leans away to look me in the eye for a moment, contemplating. He must like what he sees because his lips crush mine again.

And when I take his hand and lead it under my t-shirt, everything changes. And for the first time, I'm not afraid.

epilogue

The wedding is beautiful. A perfect Arizona day, not a cloud in the sky. The ceremony was outside at sunrise. Sandra looked absolutely beautiful. Lucas cried when my dad walked her down the aisle and I grabbed my mom's hand when her tears started falling.

Charlie held my hand through the entire ceremony.

There is obvious excitement for Sandra and Lucas, but to be honest, I think everyone is more excited I showed up. Aunts and uncles and old friends hug me and smile, telling me how great it was to see me. It was a bit overwhelming at first, but with Charlie's reassuring smile and a few deep breaths, I held it together.

His parents were the most excited to see me. His mom cried and told me how much she loved and missed me. His dad was ecstatic. He gave me such a big hug my feet lifted off the ground.

Charlie dances every slow song with me and kisses my forehead a million times.

Sandra finds me at the end of the night as she and Lucas walk through the crowd of lighters and bubbles.

She stops at the end of the line to pull me into a hug.

"I'm glad you didn't run," she whispers, gripping me tighter.

"I love you, Sandra."

She pulls away. "Thank you for coming."

I smile. "I wouldn't have missed it for anything."

"Come on, baby, let's get out of here," Lucas says, coming up behind her. She laughs as he kisses her cheek and rushes her toward the car.

Charlie whistles next to me and I wipe the tears from my cheeks as we blow bubbles toward the happy couple driving away in the car that has 'just married' written messily on the back window. We wave as they drive off and eventually the crowd disperses around me.

"Hey, you ready to go?" Charlie says, his hand placed lightly on my hip.

I look into his grey eyes that seem brighter today, a smile still on his lips.

"Thank you," I say, looping my finger into his belt loop and pulling him against me.

"What for?" he asks, his finger tracing my face.

"Everything." I smile and press my lips to his.

I'm still surprised somedays, to see how far I've come. It happens in the morning, when I wake up to the feel of his lips on cheek. It happens randomly when we're walking at the park or grocery shopping, when he takes my hand in his or guides me with his hand on my lower back and I don't cringe. My breath remains even and my vision doesn't blur. It didn't happen overnight. Sometimes he still asks my permission before he grabs my face or pulls me to him. And every time I say yes.

We haven't had sex. Charlie hasn't asked and I haven't brought it up. We've spent many hours tangled up together, hands roaming, but I haven't been able to go all the way. Charlie's been extremely patient. He doesn't get frustrated or angry. Whenever I pull away and ask him to stop, he does. He'll kiss my cheek or my forehead and hold me while I sleep. I know he wants more, I want more too. But I'm just not there yet. We both know it will happen eventually. If there is anyone I can trust with my body, it's Charlie.

He's the only boy I've ever been able to give my heart to.

Charlie smiles as he pulls away from me, telling me he'll grab my purse and be right back.

"It was beautiful, wasn't it?" my mom says, taking Charlie's place beside me, my dad coming to stand on the other side of me.

"It really was," I say as she puts her arm around my shoulders.

"I'm glad you came."

"Me too."

"Are you okay?" my dad asks.

I think before I answer.

It's the most beautiful time of day - sunset. There is no sunset like an Arizona sunset. They used to be my favorite thing about living here. Charlie and I often hiked Brown Mountain at night just to watch the sunset. Over the years, I told myself that the sunset wasn't any different in Arizona than anywhere else. Just another way I convinced myself leaving was the right thing. But standing here now, watching the sky shimmer with every color in the rainbow, my parents on either side of me, my mom's arm around me, I can't help but smile. Smile because of how far I've come. Smile because I've finally come *home.*

"Yeah, I am," I smile, and he kisses my forehead.

And when Charlie comes back, my pink purse in his hand and a grin on his face, nothing has ever felt more like home.

I spent all of my adult life running. Running away from Charlie, my parents, my sister, my fears, men, my *life.* I spent all my time afraid. Afraid that I would fail. Afraid if I let people in, they'd see just how broken I really was. I pushed everyone away so terrified that if they saw every part of me, they'd run away. So, I ran before they could. But it's all those people who you're so afraid to let see your broken pieces who need to see them.

Because in the end, they're the ones that will put you back together.

acknowledgements

First and foremost, I have to thank my family. Thank you to my parents for teaching me everything I know and constantly encouraging me to follow my many, many dreams. A huge thanks to my sisters for being the best friends a girl could ask for. To my editor/oldest sister, for being loving, supportive, encouraging...and brutally honest. To my niece and nephews who constantly remind me what real, honest, true love feels like. And lastly, to my Heavenly Father. Who has given me more blessings than I possibly deserve.

about the author

Kennie Mae Evvie was born and raised in California and has a degree in music. She learned how to tell stories through music and quickly fell in love with the power of words. She currently resides in Arizona where she spends most of her time playing with her niece and nephews, baking cakes, playing music, and dreaming of fictional men.

KEEP IN TOUCH

@kenniemaewrites